BUSCADERO

The bounty-hunting gunhawk, Buscadero, promised his dying pard, Davey Yates, that he would find his daughter, Betsy, and give her her inheritance. It meant returning to the hometown he'd left at the age of fifteen when his parents were killed on their farmstead. The infamous Maddison brothers had taken over his former home, and Buscadero discovers that Betsy is being held there. He calls in his friend, Marshal Jack Calorhan, and together they devise a plan to exterminate the nest of rustlers.

Books by Tex Larrigan
in the Linford Western Library:

BUCKMASTER
AND THE CATTLELIFTERS
BUCKMASTER

TEX LARRIGAN

BUSCADERO

Complete and Unabridged

LINFORD
Leicester

First published in Great Britain in 1991 by
Robert Hale Limited
London

First Linford Edition
published February 1994
by arrangement with
Robert Hale Limited
London

British Library CIP Data

Larrigan, Tex
    Buscadero.—Large print ed.—
Linford western library
I. Title II. Series
823.914 [F]

ISBN 0–7089–7496–1

00022 4332

Published by
F. A. Thorpe (Publishing) Ltd.
Anstey, Leicestershire

Set by Words & Graphics Ltd.
Anstey, Leicestershire
Printed and bound in Great Britain by
T. J. Press (Padstow) Ltd., Padstow, Cornwall

This book is printed on acid-free paper

1

"**Y**OU'RE a bloody idiot!" his mind howled as he leapt from the upper window landing on the water-butt below and then sprawling on the dirt of the roadway. He rolled, looking up at the exposed luscious beauty of the woman leaning out of the window in a froth of red satin and black lace.

He mourned the lost opportunity for he was a red-blooded male. He licked his lips.

"Carrie, if you would only listen to me . . ."

"Bastard! I should kill you!" Her voice was strong and clear but there was no one out there on the sidewalk to listen. The male population and those passing through were doing what all thirsty sweat-weary men did on Saturday nights. They were tending

1

their own business in one of the three main saloons in the small town that had mushroomed with the coming of the railroad spur. Greenwater Spring got its name from the oozy puddle of water that bubbled up half a mile off the main Chisholm Trail.

The man gazed up at the sight of bare flesh, the two bouncy melons practically pouring out of the restraining lace, and shook his head. The sight was better than any he'd seen in his dreams. He regretted his big mouth. If only he'd kept it shut until afterwards! Now it looked as if he'd never Buscadero know what Carrie could do for a man.

She lifted the small derringer and deliberately took careful aim. It damn well looked as if she was gunning for his vital parts! He cursed and moved fast just as she triggered. Trust a whore to go for the important bits! It figured.

She fired again, the bullets humming like bees, plunking into the dirt causing a miniature dust storm. It was time to split the breeze.

2

"Now git! And don't come back, and if you do, don't mention Betsy Yates! She ain't kinda popular in these parts!"

She slammed down the window and drew the curtains while down below beyond the batwings of the El Dorado saloon the raucous shouts and drunken laughter mingled with the tinny music of the old out-of-tune piano. The gunshots disturbed no one.

The man they called Buscadero stood up, tested his body gingerly for broken bones, found none but sundry bruises, grinned and reached for his dusty black stetson of questionable age. Dusting it off, he jammed it down hard on the thatch of coarse black hair at a jaunty angle.

So much for the ripe and lovely Carrie Smithers!

He would have to find someone else to ask about the young girl, Betsy Yates . . .

For several moments he stood cogitating. He had three choices. He could go back to the Shorthorn saloon farther down the street and ask around. Maybe someone else had come into the saloon for a late drink who might know about Betsy, or he could go and fill up at the chink's restaurant. His guts were grumbling mightily for an inch-thick steak with all the trimmings. Or he could go straight to what was supposed to be the best hotel in Greenwater Spring and find the small room he'd taken for the night and deposit the little roll of bills he'd promised to deliver from a dying man to his daughter.

Knowing the kind of men who hung around the cattle yards, he didn't fancy being bushwacked for someone else's money.

It had seemed an easy chore to promise Dave Yates to find Betsy and give her his sole wealth of seventy-four dollars and sixty-five cents. Not much after living nearly fifty years. But then many men had died worth only their boots and saddles and the stinking clobber on their backs. Dave had been lucky, if you can call being drunk and trigger-happy, lucky. Some sensitive soul hadn't liked his brand of humour and had shot him before his befuddled brains worked fast enough to pull a trigger.

But he'd lived long enough to tell his old pal Buscadero the secret he'd carried for six years. Dave had a daughter living at Greenwater Spring about three hung miles south of Abilene.

He'd promised Dave and then buried him, and then lit out from the place called Little Rock before the sheriff emerged rom a whisky haze to question the whys and wherefores of the death of Dave's killer, he being an upright citizen and on the town council.

Asking around for Betsy Yates should have been easy. The fool girl should have been living a good and quiet life as a maid for the local schoolmarm as Dave remembered her. What the hell had gone wrong? Why was Betsy Yates unpopular? And why should the most poplar madam in those parts get her rag out when the girl's name was mentioned? This puzzle was going to take some solving.

Buscadero made up his mind. To hell with it. He was going to do his stomach a favour. The wad of greenbacks he stuffed well down into a breast pocket. He'd defended his back before. He could do it again.

He walked down the deserted street, the smell of beef off the hoof and sizzling drawing him along, his guts sending messages. He hoped the chink would also have a pecan pie . . .

The vicious whine of a bullet narrowly missing his right cheek made him jump into a crouch, the explosion from a Colt forty-five coming seconds later. Some stupid bastard had either been too excited when he'd drawn a bead on him, or he was a damned bad shooter!

His right leg forward, he was ready to twist either way. He made himself into as small a target as possible. Then as another bullet sped spitefully by he located the gunman's hiding place. The bastard was hiding behind the horse-trough in front of the smithy.

A half-moon glinted on the barrels of his twin Colts. He snapped off two shots in the general direction of the shadowy trough. He heard rather than saw the movement, and this time stood tall, firing with both hands in a cross hail of bullets which he'd perfected and found so effective in more serious gun battles.

Another shot which went wild. Buscadero grinned. This clumsy gink was playing games. He must think he was aiming at a bean tin!

He automatically counted his own shots. Another burst and he would have to find a wolf lair or improvise one while he reloaded. But the problem did not arise. Another burst and there was a yelp and the sound of a body falling with a splash into the trough. Now the blacksmith isn't going to like his water polluted, Buscadero thought with a grin. But that wasn't to happen either. There was a splashing and a cursing and someone struggled out of the long metal trough and ran in a rather staggery fashion down a narrow alleyway.

Buscadero thrust his guns back in leather. He wasn't going to pursue his assailant. He wanted food. He could guess what had happened. Some misguided fool persuaded by Carrie Smithers and probably the promise of free lust had come hunting him to do the job Carrie hadn't been able to do herself. She'd chosen badly. Whoever he was wouldn't be able to hit a spitoon at six paces, not even with lungsful of spit.

He was whistling when he entered the cafe and paused to take stock in the doorway. No one he'd seen before. He was amused. The customers had all stopped eating and were watching him.

They had good reason to. Six feet four and built like an ox and all dressed

8

in black. No shiny buttons or badges to be used as a target. Black shirt and bandanna, tied down sixguns hung low enough for a smooth hand grip and the look and air of a man who'd killed. The strong dark face was battle-scarred showing like a map of rough desert above a bushy black beard. The signs of long dusty travel were on him and he smelt of horse shit and human sweat gone bad. An onlooker wouldn't have been far wrong if he'd bet that his jeans would stand up for themselves, stiffened by hardwon grease.

He knew he needed a bath. It didn't take the hint of wrinkled noses of the two dudes all tricked out in fancy store gear to make him aware of it.

"You want to express an opinion, feller?" he asked the older and bigger jasper who was in the midst of murdering his beer, while the younger shadow scraped his plate clean.

Buscadero leaned with both hands square on the table, making the first man look up at him.

9

"Do I need to?" he replied evenly. "You announced yourself ten paces outside that door! There should be a law about men like you eating in a public place. Some folk might think the meat was off!"

Buscadero swooped forward and grasped the man's fancy collar and gave it a twist, making the dude hawk and gag. The younger man made as to get up. Buscadero downed him with his other hand, which unfortunately for the youth was holding his Colt. The sharp rap silenced any protest he was about to make.

"I don't take your kind of bullshit from any man," he rasped, and flung the dude back in his chair. There was a mighty crack as the wooden chairback gave and the man crashed back on to the floor.

Buscadero stood over him, his breath hardly quickened.

"I'm mean when I'm hungry and you thank your stars I'm not gut-starving. Now an apology for that sniff and we'll call it quits and no offence."

"Apologise? Do you know who're you talking to, buster?"

"No, and I don't care, feller. You could be the governor of this state and I wouldn't care a shit!"

"I'm Joss K. Maddison and the boy you've pistol-whipped is my brother Paul. The Maddisons don't forget insults, buster!"

Buscadero shrugged.

"You want to try your hand?" His tone was soft and silky, and suddenly dinner plates were pushed away and several diners left in a hurry as if they'd just remembered other pressing appointments. The others got out of the line of fire.

The dude's face paled and Buscadero's lips curled.

"Cain't do your own shooting, uh? Gotta tribe of gunhawks to do the business for you? What about the kid here? Does he play with a peashooter?"

The youth raised angry eyes at the

black-clad gunman and struggled to rise.

"Why, you . . . " and his brother gave him a vicious punch in the chest as Buscadero's gun cleared leather. The two men glared at each other.

"He's only a hot-headed boy," the man said through clenched teeth. Buscadero nodded.

"I know. I've been through the piss-proud days, mister. I wouldn't have shot him, just close enough to make him wet his pants! Now about that apology."

Joss K. licked his lips and looked around the restaurant at the interested faces remaining. It would be all over town. Joss K. Maddison knuckling down to a saddle-tramp! Anger burned within him.

"I'm sorry, mister. Any guy travelling distances could smell just as sweet . . . "

"Louder, feller. I'll relish my victuals better if these here folk who's curious about this outcome can hear your apology loud and clear. Then when they go around this here little ol' town they can tell the truth of the matter to those waitin' to know!"

For a moment it looked as if Maddison was considering his chances. Then he looked at the hardware and where it was carried and his heart failed him.

"What's your name, buster?"

"Buscadero," and there was a stifled gasp that rippled round the big room. Even the chink stopped polishing glasses to look at the big man.

Buscadero smiled. His reputation had preceded him.

"Now about that apology? Make it loud and clear."

Maddison choked. "I'M SORRY, MR BUSCADERO. I HAVE A COLD IN THE HEAD. I MERELY SNIFFED BECAUSE OF IT."

There was a titter in the far corner of the restaurant and Maddison glared. Then he got up roughly from the table and hauled his brother upright.

"Come on Paul, let's get to hell

outta here. We've got business in the El Dorado."

The chink met them at the door with his palm outstretched. Maddison tossed him some coins, some of which rolled on the floor, and left the black-clad chink scrabbling on his knees.

"And when you've finshed down there," Buscadero called, "bring me the biggest steak you've got in the place and all the trimmings and if you've got pie, I'll have two helpings, and while I'm waiting I'll take some coffee."

"Yes, suh! Coming up right away, suh!" and the grinning chink pocketed his coins and scuttled away, his soft flipflop slippers slapping the wooden floor.

The chink proved a good cook and the food settled the last feelings of irritation. When he paid Lee Fong, he said softly.

"Do I smell?" The yellow face went putty-grey, the grin slipping to a worried frown.

"Well . . . " The chink coughed and sighed.

"'Nuff said. Where's the nearest bath-house and barber?"

"Three doors along. Always hot water and he good barber. Yes suh!"

"Then thanks, old man. I'll be back," and Buscadero strode from the restaurant.

It was after a long leisurely bath, during which one of Jimmy Protheroe's bath-house water-carriers nipped off and bought some new gear for Buscadero, that old Jimmy Protheroe looked down at the half-shaven face and then slapped his thigh with his free hand.

"Well, I'm damned! I know you, you sonofabitch! You're Edward Juantes, son of that Mexican dirt-farmer and the travelling preacher's daughter from New England! How long is it? Fifteen years?"

"Nearer twenty." Buscadero lay back on the barber's chair and grinned. "I didn't think anyone would recognise me. Most folk are strangers around here. How've you been, Jimmy?"

"Oh, well enough. Lots of changes here and not all for the better."

"I see you're overrun with dancehalls and saloons. The El Dorado is new."

"Yeh, run by Carrie Smithers and owned by Joss K. Maddison who just about runs everything round here. Of course we've got to thank him for the spur that connects us to the main railroad. Brought lots of new business as well as the sharks. But he's power-mad, is Joss K. His word's law and his men sees that it's kept. He even owns the women . . . "

"Oh? How's that, Jimmy? Surely the usual arrangements between owners and madams is the same as anywhere else?"

"I mean more than that, bud. He thinks he owns all the women in town, respectable women as well as the other kind. He can make life hell for a woman if she doesn't give him what he wants."

"Sounds a right bastard. Have there

been many women who've refused him?"

"A handful. Two had husbands who objected and they were shot. Joss K. fixed it for one of his gunmen to challenge them and killed them in fair fight. So nothing came of the killings. Another respectable woman suffered a ridicule campaign. It was rumoured she was really a feller and that was why she posed as a spinster. She up stakes and left to go back east even though she was making a good living as a schoolmarm. It was even rumoured she kept a pretty little maid for fun and games. She disappeared too. No one knows where the hell she took herself off to."

"She wasn't called Betsy Yates?"

Jimmy was just drying off Buscadero's newly shaved face. He paused, and looked down at his client.

"How the hell did you know that? She came to town long after you left."

Buscadero's strong white teeth showed in a grin and Jimmy felt uncomfortable.

It was like looking at one of them sable wolves eyeball to eyeball. He blinked. Buscadero. The word meant gunhawk in Mexican. This wasn't the same Edward Juantes who'd left Greenwater Spring twenty years ago at fifteen. The boy who'd been broken-hearted on the violent death of his parents and cowed by the man who'd ordered the killing . . .

"I rode with her father for years. We had some wild times. He taught me everything I should know to remain alive. But he fell for the oldest trick in the book. He was bushwacked, drawn into an alley because he thought I needed help. But before he died he told me about this daughter, Betsy. He'd deserted her. But he said it was for the girl's own good. He left her with a schoolmarm . . . "

"Aye, Susie Mcgear. She's the one who upstakes and left and the town lost a good teacher, and all because of that rat, Joss K. Maddison."

"What about this story that all the

18

town hates Betsy? I was in the El Dorado asking around and this lovely ripe peach of a woman called Carrie Smithers took me upstairs with other things on her mind. I hadn't even got my shirt off when I opened my fool mouth and asked her about Betsy. She exploded and pulled out an itsy-bitsy gun and was waving it about like she couldn't make up her mind up where to plug me. While she make up her mind I dived outta the window, her screaming about killing me and not to mention Betsy Yates again. Betsy Yates were two dirty words. What gives?"

Jimmy shrugged bony shouders, face suddenly closed up.

"They say she was enticing kids to the house. She was also blamed for taking Joss away from Carrie. He stopped seeing Carrie except on rare occasions and Carrie got it into her head that little Betsy Yates was his secret lover. It stands to reason someone was taking up his time. He wasn't whoring around as much. But the whisper had it that

19

Betsy was procuring both boys and girls for him, which to me is a load of bollocks! Betsy loved kids and Susie Mcgear was training her to become as good a teacher as she was herself."

"But the children would be able to deny it to their parents?"

"The whisper got out that kids were denying it to protect Betsy and our parson has been preaching fire and brimstone against poor Betsy. No one dare speak of her these days."

"And no one knows where she's gone?"

Jimmy shook his head. "I've got ideas but it pays not to talk round here. Joss K.'s ears are everywhere."

The man in black stood up and peered into the spotted mirror and rubbed a calloused hand over his smooth chin. He saw a lean jaw, the skin stretched tautly over craggy cheeks. He looked more Mexican than American, his mother's genes overwhelmed by the stronger passionate Mexican's. The nose was strong but slightly bent from a brawl way back in the days before he had sense to keep his eyes open in his arse. He noted new lines and grooves that hadn't been there the last time he shaved. He pondered. Every year of his thirty-five years was there on his face and a few more besides. At the rate he was going he'd be an old man before he was forty.

It wasn't an attractive face. He didn't like it himself. It was enough to frighten babies and the shit out of old men. But there was power and a whole lot of grieving in that face. It was the only one he had. He had to make the best of it.

"You did a great job. How much for the bath and the shave? And give that swamper of yours a dollar for getting duds that fit."

"What about ten dollars?" Buscadero's eyebrows rose. Jimmy hurriedly changed his mind. This guy might have, twitchy fingers. "Make it seven, for old times' sake."

"Thanks, Jimmy. I'll not forget."

Buscadero's smile was mild. Jimmy relaxed and thought he could give this Juantes boy something for free.

"Somehing you should know, Edward."

"Yeh, what is it?"

"Joss K. Maddison is the son of the man who run you Mexes off the land. He's living on the site that was your old place. I thought you should know."

2

HE was conscious of a searing pain closely followed by hate and an over-riding anger. He was trembling when he walked outside into the glare of the sun. Not many times he'd experienced the naked pain and passion as he did now. Once, it had happened when he watched Davey Yates die, and he'd gone in with guns blazing and wiped out a scorpions nest. He'd got a couple of bullet scars as mementoes from that little lot. But he carried them with pride.

He flexed his muscles. He had an itch in his fingers. Maybe he would take a ride out to the old rancheria and take himself a looksee. It would be quite something to wander over the land he'd known as a wide-eyed kid.

He rode quietly out of town. He knew by the spine-tingling niggle in his back that eyes watched him go. But to hell with it, if anyone wanted to play games with him, he could accommodate them when he returned.

The old trail reminded him of things long forgotten. There was the big rock standing clear up to heaven and always in the clouds. His New England mother had queer fancies. She'd said it was the heavenly gateway itself. One climbed up there and one could get a glimpse of what was to come. Ma had taken her religion seriously despite the fact she'd run away from a strict father who was a fire-and-brimstone preacher. Over the years, he'd wondered what had happened to his old grandpa. Strange to think he had a relative somewhere on this earth.

He recalled his father. He was the one who'd called him Eduardo. Funny really. They'd been good parents but they'd always disagreed about how to pronounce his name. But Edward or Eduardo, he answered to both and he'd got Ed at the little school in

Greenwater Spring. In those days it was run by the widow of a sheriff who'd come on hard times, and she took her fee in vegetables and oats and the odd rib of beef, depending on what folks had to offer. He couldn't recall what kind of teacher she was, but she sure could wield a cane!

He reined his roan at the rim of the little valley. The trail was the same but deeper rutted. A stand of cottonwoods had gone, no doubt cut down to build the elaborate ranch-house and the barns and bunkhouses below. They were built in a square like a miniature fort and beyond them were the corrals. He could see several horses loose in one of the corrals and in the other a tall pole with a contraption for use in breaking in young stock.

As he watched he saw a limping white-aproned figure cross the yard. It looked as if Joss K. Maddison employed a man as cook for the men in the bunkhouse. He had a pail in his hand and the watching man's eyes narrowed. The same old well was in use. He'd helped his father dig that well and build the adobe wall around it. He'd been pleased and proud when his father praised him.

"Someday you're going to quite a man, my Eduardo!" A tear glistened in his eye and he hastily brushed it away. Buscadero weeping? Jesus! That would be the day!

He moved to the shadow of the rocks and knowing of a crevice from long ago, he tied up his roan in the shade and made his way carefully below. He had no notion of what he was going to do. He just wanted the layout of the place, to brood about what might have been. If his parents had been alive, maybe their ranch would have looked something like this. He had this urge to torture himself.

It was a form of grieving. He'd locked out thoughts of his loss years ago when he was a boy. It had been the only way to survive, but it had been a hollow thing. It was as if the juice of life had died within him. He'd been conscious of a ruthless streak in him that had driven him on. He'd had no conscience. It didn't matter which side he was working for as long as they paid. He'd done things in the past he could be ashamed of if he allowed himself to think of it. He'd bounty-hunted for the law and taken contracts for victims to be shot because they were above the law and could not be touched. He'd also taken the greenbacks from some of the most powerful gang bosses back east. He'd acted as professional exterminator and the acts themselves hadn't touched his soul.

The only thing that worried him was the size of the fee and if it would be paid.

The flaring anger experienced when the only person in the world who cared whether he lived or died was shot, opened up sensations he thought didn't exist in him. Davey Yates had been many things to him: father, mentor, best friend and sometimes even the conscience he wasn't aware of himself.

Buscadero, the man coming back to Greenwater Spring, wasn't quite the man known as the man with invisible hands. A chink of human feeling was letting in the light into a soul not quite black.

Greenwater Spring was hurrying along the process, and the flood of memories never allowed, until now, to invade his mind.

He would deal with Joss K. Maddison because he was his father's son.

But first he had to find Betsy Yates and give her Davey's legacy and where better than to visit Joss K. Maddison on his home ground and ask about Susie Mcgear and what happened to both women.

His mind made up, he climbed back to where his horse was tethered. He took his time. He cleaned both guns with an oily rag he carried for the purpose in his warbag and finished with ten minutes of handling both guns. Satisfied with the fast draws he twirled both weapons and they seemed to leap of their own accord back into leather.

He loaded up the repeating rifle thrust deep in the scabbard on the mettlesome roan. A few muttered words soothed the beast who then rubbed his head against his shoulder.

"All right, you doggone sonofabitch, we'll get going. I know you don't like standing around, not since that mountain cat nearly had you for breakfast! Come on, we'll go and see what reaction we can get out of the great Joss K. Maddison."

They picked their way down the widened trail which he could see had been strengthened and rebuilt where the ground had slipped during some long-gone wet season. He saw that his presence had been noted. Someone down below was watching, a winchester slung nonchalantly over his left arm. Coming nearer, he saw it was the youth, Paul Maddison, all decked out like a dude in fancy shirt and red and yellow bandanna. His stetson was white . . . hadn't anyone told the fool that his bandanna and hat made great targets for anyone having reason to bushwack him? Someday the snotty kid would find out the hard way.

"Hi, there, your brother home?"

"Who wants to know?"

"Don't you remember me, kid?" The boy's eyes widened. He didn't expect anyone crossing his brother would have the nerve and the gall to come looking for him on his home ground, what with boys backing him up and all.

"You're the feller who made my brother apologise in front of those townsmen! Jeese! I don't know what he's going to say about this!"

Buscadero smiled his wolfish grin. "Then you'd better go and find out, hadn't you, buster?"

The boy scowled. "Who're you calling buster? My name's Paul Maddison, I'll have you know."

"You're still a snotty-nosed kid!"

"Yuh bugger, I should . . . "

"I shouldn't if I were you," and suddenly to the boy's fascinated gaze, a forty-five Colt seemed to materialise in a steady hand and it was pointing straight at his heart. "Now kid, I don't aim to spill your gore but I will if I have to. Now just turn round nice and slow and shout for your brother and tell him to come peaceable or you'll get a nasty itch between the shoulder-blades."

The boy turned slowly and suddenly he was straddle-legged and Buscadero grinned widely.

"There sure is a bad smell around here. Now call him loud and clear and make no mistakes and if you're a good boy I'll let you go and change your diaper!"

The boy didn't have to whistle up his voice. Joss K. Maddison came slowly out of the front door and stood on the verandah. His look was glowering.

"I heard you, stranger. You're the guy in the chink's place. I oughta . . . "

As if by magic the Colt was once again in the man in black's hand and this time trained on Joss K. Maddison's forehead. Buscadero leaned forward over his horse's pommel. "One move, mister, and I'll blow you to hell!"

Maddison's hands crept high. They were visibly shaking. Buscadero's lips curled. Here was a man who relied on others to do his bidding. His eyes raked the nearby buildings but no one and nothing moved. Maybe he'd caught Maddison flatfooted and his men out on the range except for the old cook. He frowned. Even a crippled cook could cause devastation if he had a shotgun.

"Where's Cookie? Call him. We've gotta talk, Maddison, and I don't want to be distracted by an old coot waiting to cover himself in glory."

"He's in the bunkhouse."

"Who else have you got inside your house?" He saw Maddison's eyes flicker and the boy Paul moved uneasily until Buscadero's gun wavered between the two brothers. "Goddamit! Who's inside?"

Maddison seemed to have difficulty in swallowing.

"Just a Mex housekeeper."

"She cook too?"

"Yeh. Makes a damn hot chilli."

Suddenly Buscadero make up his mind. This talk would be safer inside. He didn't want any of Maddison's riders coming in off the range during the exciting bits. He climbed down from his horse wrapping the reins over the hitching rein and and at the same time grabbing the paralysed Paul by the upper arm.

"We'll talk inside," he said tersely and propelled the reluctant boy up the verandah steps. "Any false move, Maddison, and your brother gets it."

Maddison stepped back and into the house, white-faced and watchful. His raised right hand twitched as if he couldn't control the urge to go for his gun.

Buscadero smiled.

"Go on, do it. Go for our gun!"

Maddison stared at him. "Just who

33

are you? You act as if you know me and I'm not talking about what happened in that goddamn eatery."

Buscadero laughed with amusement showing the strong white teeth that gave him that wolfish look. It turned his sinister ugly face into that of a professional killer.

"If you knew that, I'd be giving you an advantage I sure don't want you to have. Just let's say I'm a friend of Betsy Yates' father. Now what I want to know, where is she? And I want no bullshit, Maddison."

The man backed away, his eyes focused on the black muzzle of the gun trained on his midriff. Buscadero sniffed.

"Now don't waste my time, mister. This brother of yours offends me. He smells worse than a sty full of pigs!"

"Why you . . . " Maddison's face turned red. He jerked forward and then back as the gun finger tightened on the trigger. He relaxed and his dry tongue licked round dry lips.

"Enough of this shit, Maddison. Where is she?"

"I don't know who you're talking about!" Buscadero was conscious of the boy Paul giving his brother a sharp glance. It caused a tingle up his spine.

"You're lying, mister. You know Betsy Yates. Used to work for the schoolmarm you hounded outta Greenwater Spring. She wouldn't let you have your wicked way with her. Now where's Betsy for the last time . . ." and he raised the Colt slowly and took aim at a glass dome that held a cluster of white wax flowers. It shattered into a thousand shards splattering Maddison, one splinter narrowly missing his eye and digging itself into his cheek. He pulled it out and a trickle of blood ran down past his mouth and dripped on to the crisp check shirt.

"You bastard . . . I'll get you for this."

Buscadero's lips twitched. "I'm no bastard and I've got the papers to prove it. I could shoot you for insulting my mother, but for this time I want you alive. One last time, Maddison."

"I tell you, I don't know! She was one of them queer ones. Went off with the schoolmarm, I expect. God knows where either of them are now, but one thing's certain, they'll be together. I swear it!"

Buscadero could feel the rigid arm of Paul Maddison relax. The young fool had a knowing smile on his face as if he knew something funny. It triggered the meanness that was always lying just under the surface of Buscadero's consciousness.

"What's funny, kid? Is that brother of yours feeding me shit?"

The boy suddenly looked frightened.

"I don't know what you mean . . . "

"Keep your mouth shut, Paul, or I'll skin you alive!" Joss K. Maddison's face was suffused with angry colour. Paul looked from one to the other. He couldn't decide which man he was more frightened of.

Buscadero tightened his grip on the boy's arm until he screamed in a high-pitched schoolboy squeak. Then Buscadero eased the pressure.

"Now boy, just tell me what you know. Your brother threatens to skin you alive. That's a maiden's teaparty to what I can do to you if I put my mind to it. I once remember frying a guy's balls and the gristly bit and making him eat them but I can't remember whether he enjoyed them or not. Probably didn't because we had no salt . . . Then there was the old feller who tried bushwacking me. He was old, so he got off more lightly than a young feller like you. I just staked him out in the desert and cut off his eyelids . . . Oh, I could go on all day telling you of some of my favourite techniques." His voice dropped and he whispered gently in the terrified boy's ear. "Where's Betsy?"

The boy's blue eyes were drowned in tears. He stared up at Buscadero like a jackrabbit hypnotised by a snake.

"She's outback. Tied up . . . "

"PAUL! DAMN YOUR HIDE . . . !"

A shot from the doorway blasted the eardrums. Buscadero whirled as the bullet went wild. His automatic crouch covered the swift action of pulling the second gun. The cook managed to fire for the second time when two shots with barely seconds between them slammed into his chest. Blood spurted and, with a surprised look, the old man slumped to the ground.

The boy had been flung on his back and was struggling to rise. Out of the corner of his eye, Buscadero saw Maddison fumbling for his gun from a table drawer. His body moved smoothly. The shot took Maddison in the shoulder. Buscadero was not even breathing quickly. He blew both barrels and leathered them, secure in the knowledge that he could out-shoot them or anybody else who interfered with the business in hand.

He jerked the boy upright and then

hauled the groaning Maddison to his feet.

"Take me to her now or I'll finsh the job off!"

They went outside and out into the yard to an old dugout shed that Buscadero remembered. His mother had used it as a storehouse. He remembered his father telling him that it was one of the first jobs his mother made him do. It was cool and roomy with a dirt floor and without light for there were no windows.

Maddison produced a large key and unlocked the padlock and threw the heavy door open. Rickety wooden steps led down. Buscadero pushed them both down before him. Paul stumbled and fell knocking his brother down with him. They sprawled in the dirt.

There was the sour smell of beer and rotten apples and the human smell of someone living there twenty-four hours a day without the facilities for bathing. There was also the smell of chilli.

Buscadero waited until his eyes

adjusted from the outside glare to that of the dimness now possible from the open door.

"Betsy Yates? Are you there?" and a choked voice mumbled and a drumming noise as if someone's heels beat on the floor.

Buscadero stepped round a huge pickling vat and found Betsy Yates crouched low on a straw palliasse. She was gagged and fastened by a chain around her neck to a staple in the wall. Her movements were restricted to the use of a bucket and she could just turn and lie down. Two bowls of food and a jug of tepid water were on the floor beside her. Just like a kennelled dog, Buscadero thought with detached fury.

Her eyes glinted up at him with sudden fear and shock. He smiled but it didn't reassure her. It might be from the frying pan into the fire. He untied her gag and then fumbled at her neck. The chain needed a key to untie the lock.

He grabbed up Maddison regardless of his wound.

"Where's the key?" he grated. Maddison pointed wordlessly to the wall. The key hung on a nail. He flung Maddison with some violence to the wall which he hit with a spine-numbing crash. He slid down unconscious, his wound spouting blood. The boy groaned. He'd twisted an ankle. Swiftly Buscadero loosed the chain and picked the girl up and climbed the stairs. Then dumping her on the ground he closed and locked the storehouse door and then threw away the key. That would give the riders something to think about, he thought with grim humour.

He looked at the girl. She was a stinking mess, hair unkempt and her clothes torn as if she'd been ravaged by wolves. He'd half a mind to open up and go back and shoot the bastard right now. But he knew that a quick death was too good for the bastard. It was going to take time and thought on the fate of Joss K. Maddison.

There was a tantalysing familiarity about the man, triggered off by Maddison's own words. He'd sensed something before the man spoke but the tone of voice, the timbre, rang a bell. He sensed again something elusive, just at the back of his mind. It irked him. It was as if he should remember something he'd forgotten. To hell with it. He'd figure it later.

The first thing was to get this girl back to civilisation and then find out her story. He would take her to Jimmy, the barber and his swamper could nip out and buy the girl some duds to make her respectable again. She would be quite a good looker if she was washed and combed. He didn't mind the free view of dirty rosy-tipped nipples. In fact he quite enjoyed it, but he knew women set much store on their respectability and as far as he knew Davey Yates' daughter wasn't a whore.

There was the sound of distant

rifle fire. A slug scudded dangerously close and splintered the sun-dried planks of what smelled like a pig's shithouse. There was no time to ponder. Back there, coming down the valley lickety-spit were three of Maddison's gunhawks, one of whom was already crouched over his rifle figuring on a better aim.

"Shit!" and Buscadero scooped up the still sun-blinded girl and flung her over his shoulder and set out on a diving weaving lope to reach his tethered horse. She was no mean weight for a little 'un, and it took grim determination to fling her up front on the roan's back legs astride. The roan repaid those lonely nights when they'd camped in remote wildernesses and he'd had no one to talk to or care for. The roan had claimed all his attention and he and the gelding shared a trust that it would be hard to break. The roan stood still as the strange human lump was dumped aboard. Then, feeling the second heave-ho, and the urgent rowelling in the ribs, the mighty horse leapt away in the opposite direction from which the riders were fast descending.

It was fortunate that Buscadero knew every inch of this land. He'd hunted and shot over it and helped till part of it since the first time he'd forked a horse. He angled away from the obvious trail into the far hills and made for a stretch of barren wasteland that he guessed Maddison and his men would only visit when rounding up stock. A quick glance as he rode showed the old fields neglected and in some cases the crude timber and wire fences torn down. Maddison had not taken advantage of his father's labour. It was now an enclosed ranch with more steers to the acre than he'd ever remembered. There were also a couple of herds of horses, small units, and each had several foals following at heel. For the first time Buscadero wondered what Maddison's real business was. There wasn't enough stock to warrant his struggle for the big power stakes and yet the townsfolk allowed him to run all over them.

Maddison and his outfit could sure do with investigating before he allowed himself the luxury of settling old debts. Maybe the girl would know all about big man Maddison.

The roan, strong and leggy as he was, was tiring. The going had been rough and ever up a long slow slope. Buscadero knew exactly where he was heading. A lonely cleft in a jutting crag where he'd bedded down as a boy. It was one of the few places in this dusty dry landscape where a small spring struggled to surface. It wasn't always wet, not in very droughty times, but often as not the pool held enough water for a man and his horse to drink. It had always been a jealously guarded secret when his father was alive. They kept it covered over with slabs of stone and left only a small uncovered section for the wild animals to drink. It was better that way or those same animals would have scratched out the pool and maybe have kept it exposed for any curious rider to find. He hoped this was not the case.

There was little sign that men on horseback ever came this way. He took his time and allowed the roan to find his own way. A little later, the horse's ears pricked. He could smell water. He nickered and Buscadero's hand patted his neck.

"Not so far now, old buddy. You deserve a good drink and if the old place is still the same there'll be some grass growing nearby."

Nostalgia hit him. He hadn't expected it for wasn't he a coldhearted killer who relied on the fast reflex of hand and eye to earn his living? Anger and hate and the hope of revenge plus the unaccustomed thinking about his parents and his childhood had softened something that had been ice-bound for so long.

He remembered the fifteen year-old boy who'd ridden away from the burned-out farm, the laughing-stock of the elder Maddison's bunch of men. The jeers and jibes and the gunshots drawing dust from his poor old pony's heels. He'd bottled up the shame along with the grief. He'd been a poor ignorant farmer's boy whose only experience with the outside world was his Saturday night visit to Greenwater Spring. There, he'd found he liked the taste of the local beer and liked looking at the fancy women.

Twenty years later, he knew more about drinking and the women. He also knew about men. He'd ridden many dusty trails, tried many varied jobs from lumberjacking in Canada to trailing herds to the cattle-pens of Abilene and breaking horses down in New Mexico. That had been before he found the bizarre job of bounty-hunting and found he had a gift for hunting a man over long-dead trails. The name Buscadero had been hard earned. Some of the hunted objected to be taken back to Fort Smith to stand trial.

They gambled their lives against the boyish-faced half breed Mexican and died never realising that instead of spending nights with the local whores, Buscadero cleaned and oiled his guns and practised that swift nearly invisible draw to make it smooth like running water . . .

That draw, and the alert mind that went with it, saved his life on countless occasions.

He had been a cold killing instrument to do it.

Was he now at this stage of his life becoming soft? A man of jumping nerves made weak by memories so long dead?

If he was, he could now be in dead trouble. He was also very aware of the feminine bundle of trouble leaning against his chest. He swore. Nostalgia was beating the hell out of him in more ways than one.

He slid from the horse and held his hands up to help her down, eyes and body aware of soft pink skin and the rosy nipples of well rounded breasts peeping out from the torn bodice of her dress. It was very apparent that though she might have been a virgin when Maddison kidnapped her, she sure wasn't now. Her bold eyes proved it.

"What am I going to do with you?" he growled and turned away to unloosen the roan's girths and take off the saddle to allow the beast to roll.

"What we stopped here for?" the girl asked, big-eyed.

"Not for what you're thinking," he answered snappily. "There's a spring just up the rocks a piece. I'll have to go and inspect it. I hope I'll have some rocks to shift."

"Oh? You know this land then?"

"I should. I was brought up on it," he answered grimly.

"But you're not a Maddison. I've never seen you before. Besides, you wouldn't have shot up Joss and left him and that poison-prick Paul locked in that store-room."

49

Buscadero nodded. "That's right. It's a long story. I'll tell you some time."

"Just who are you? Are you as bad as the others? Are you going to rape me?"

He looked at her with narrowed eyes.

"Would it be rape?" She flushed and looked away but not before he saw the flash in her eyes. She missed the fleeting smile that passed over his craggy face. He might look a mean bastard, but he knew his influence over a certain kind of woman . . .

"I'll go look for that water. If the spring is undisturbed I know we have a good chance of a fairly quiet night . . . that is," and now she did see his smile, "that is if you want a quiet night . . . "

3

THE spring was found to be intact. It didn't look as if either Indians or white men knew of the hideaway source of water, which wasn't surprising as it nestled at the foot of a jumble of rocks which teetered on the edge of an escarpment. A winding narrow animal trail led upwards, so dangerously steep that itself must have put off any strangers exploring further. Another reason was that no grazing was visible. The small patch of lush grass around the pool was all but invisible from lower ground. Maddison's riders, if they were fool enough to come looking this way for lost steers, Buscadero decided were not loyal enough to endanger their own hides by enduring the sweltering sun and the rough riding necessary to operate on this part of the range.

It gave him the idea to rest up there instead of going onto Greenwater Spring where Maddison and his men would be surely on the lookout for him and Betsy. He led the roan up the dangerous slope, the gelding's long legs scrambling and slipping. Small rocks were dislodged. Buscadero cursed. If any curious riders came looking, those rocks would be a dead giveaway.

"Any Indian trackers down there working for Maddison?"

"No. A couple of Mexican vaqueros who look after the horses and any young calves brought in because they've lost their mothers. Otherwise there's six riders and that young shit Paul who gets up everyone's noses, and Joss won't hear a word agen him. One of these days someone is gonna put a bullet in the arrogant young bugger's back!"

"So you don't like him, huh?"

They were sitting one on each side of a small dry wood fire sheltered in the deep cave that Buscadero remembered from his boyhood. It smelled as if it had been used in recent times as a wolf den. It figured, but probably lack of animals to hunt and a growing litter had moved the family on.

"Like him? What? That little prick? You must be joking. He'll grow up into a mean sadistic monster . . . if he lives long enough. Just see what he did to me," and she pulled up her skirt to her knees and showed him the rows of cigarette burns running up the inside of both thighs.

Buscadero's breath drew in, in a sharp hiss. He was a hard man and he'd once shot a woman, but she'd been more of a man than a woman, but even so, he didn't like thinking about it. But it had been necessary. But this . . . no excuse could justify deliberate torture.

"And did Maddison let him get away with it?" The girl shrugged her shoulders, the shirt Buscadero had flung her earlier slipping showing part of a smooth shoulder. She was a whole sight cleaner now, not quite smell-less

53

but enough to show how attractive she could be on a good day.

"He'd had his leg over. He didn't care what happened after that. He thought it was funny that Paul couldn't perform. Paul hated him laughing and he took it out of me by rolling a cigarette and alternately puffing and stubbing it on my legs. I was the whipping-boy for both of them. Joss had some funny ways too . . . I could tell you things . . . !"

"I can guess." His tone was grim. He'd met men like the Maddisons before. Power mad, and with exaggerated ideas of life and death over those who were unfortunate to be in their hands. They usually died violently. Buscadero made it his duty to dispatch those who strayed into his path. He reckoned it was his bounden duty. He chalked up another black mark for why Joss K. Maddison should face him with a gun in his hand for the last time. As for Paul . . . he was young, probably not more than seventeen. Maybe scaring him shitless again might do the trick. For sure as God made little green apples someone somewhere would do for him . . . Buscadero had a reputation to protect. He didn't kill kids still wet behind the ears.

Betsy watched him, the flickering flames between them. They cast devil-like shadows across the dark craggy features. It was a strong ruthless face and Betsy had a strong stirring within her. She was curious about what it would be like being possessed by this hard rather silent man. She would either hate it or crave for more. There would be no half-measures with this man, and he looked as if he knew well what to do and keep on doing it!

Her head on a side, she eyed him mischievously.

"You meant it when you said it might not be a quiet night?"

Buscadero paused in the act of rolling a cigarette. His guts still rumbled from the sparse meal of jerky. Only the scalding black coffee thickly sugared had escaped Betsy's grumbling. "The jerky's not fit for the buzzards" she'd said. Now she looked all perked up.

"Depends."

"On what?" She was getting a trifle edgy with this unpredictable man. He sighed.

"You're just a kid. I don't hump kids! How old are you, sixteen . . . seventeen?"

She was affronted. God knows why. He hadn't meant it as an insult. He just didn't want her to think he'd jump on any woman, even though it was plain she'd had some experience.

"Lay, off, will you? I'm trying to control my urges."

"I'm twenty! I'm not just a kid. I know what I'm doing!"

He smiled at her show of temper. He struck a match on the butt of one of his guns and lit the home made quirley and drew hard and the smoke swamped his lungs.

"So! You're twenty. Quite an old woman!"

"Look, mister, are you or aren't you?"

"Well, if you put it like that . . . you've not got much finesse."

"What's that?"

"If you don't know, you're too young to be propositioning a feller. You should wait until you're asked or do you want to be raped? Do you get your thrills that way?"

"Say, are you gooky, mister? Are you like Paul?"

She grinned when he scowled. "I'll show you if I'm like Paul or not when I'm good and ready. Don't you ever use your brains, or do you keep 'em between your legs?"

"I don't know what you mean."

"I knew it. Thick. Don't you wonder why I came charging down into that muckhole and got you out?"

For a long moment she just looked at him, then a peculiar expression crossed over her quite pretty face.

"No, I didn't. Come to mention it, why did you?"

"You're the reason I rode into Greenwater Spring. I knew your father . . . "

"Oho! You're one of them!"

"One of what?"

"A fast shooting, never-stop-in-one-place gunhawk. He's dead, isn't he? I've been expecting it for years. He says, 'Stay with the good schoolmarm, love, and I'll be back with a hat full of money and we'll buy us a little ranch . . . ' Like hell did he come back! He wasn't for settling down. Ma should never have listened to him . . . "

"What happened to her?"

"Had a baby that went wrong and no doctor within a hundred miles. Died when I was ten. If it hadn't been for Suzie Mcgear I would have starved."

Bucadero nodded. "Sounds like Dave. He had a thing about saving his money. Always talked about getting himself a big stake. Then we'd hit town for a few days and he'd drink himself silly and boast about keeping away from the green baize tables. Then when he was good and tight, some piss-proud cardsharp would give out a challenge he couldn't resist. Then he'd lose the lot and I found myself grubstaking him again. He was a fool to himself. It was the only time he nearly killed me. If he hadn't been so drunk he would have drawn first. He had a helluva draw. He taught me all I know about guns."

"Why did he nearly kill you?"

"I figured four days' drinking would just about do it. I locked him in the hotel room on the fourth night. I figured if we could get away early next morning, he'd have his roll intact. But the sonofabitch shot the lock on the door. He wasn't just tight but fighting mad. He came after me firing at my feet and I went through that goldarn hotel as if the devil was after me. Then he hit me in the arse and nicked a lump outta me which has spoiled the look of it to this day. Then he started to cry and mopped me up because I couldn't reach it myself. Then damn me if he didn't go right on down to that saloon and found a card school a-going whips and jingle! He horned in and got hisself cleaned out. You know somehing? He always reckoned he was a good poker player, but where he got that idea I don't know. Anyhow he left you seventy-four dollars and sixty-five cents and I'll be sure glad to hand it over."

"He did?" Her eyes glistened. "So he did keep his promise about the money. He meant to even if he couldn't come himself! Poor Pa. I wish he'd come back!"

"But there'd been times when he could have come back with his hat full of money as he promised! He was a fool! But a lovable fool and the best pard a feller could have."

"I don't care about what he should have done! He did think of me at the last. Did he ever talk about me?" She looked so happy, it was a shame to pull the rug.

"Well . . . er . . . sometimes, but he was a secretive man. We never talked about the future. I don't think either of us expected to have a future."

"Oh, I forgot about that part of it. Did he . . . and you, kill many men?" There was a catch of her breath.

"Look, let's talk of something else."

"What about . . . ?" and she winked.

"Well, seeing as you're twenty . . . You're not giving me no lies?"

"I'd show you Ma's journal. There's an entry and a date when I popped into the world, but I've forgotten it and I lost the book it was in. Now do you believe me?"

"Doesn't seem to matter," and he moved round the dying fire and sat close, an arm going about her shoulders.

"You've yet got to prove you're not like Paul . . . "

"And I said I'd show you."

And he did!

4

"WOW!"
She looked up at him and stretched like the cat that had drunk all the cream and licked out the bowl too.

"Get dressed, it's nearly dawn. We'll split the breeze before Maddison's crew realises we're gone."

"Say, you're quite a man. You're nothing like Joss Maddison or that ramrod Cal Emmett. I didn't think it could be like that."

"So! You're not too old to learn something. Now if you want to take a leak or something, get on with it. You can chew jerk on the trail. Remember, this horse is riding double and if we run into them it could be pearly gates time. I don't think Mr Maddison will take into account you maybe stopping a bullet in the circumstances."

She shivered, suddenly all her outer bravery shattered. She was just a frightened girl.

"He wanted me to live with him freely and openly but I wouldn't. The more I defied him, the more brutal he became until . . . " Suddenly she was clinging to him and weeping stormily. "I never dreamed men could be so like animals!"

"There now." Buscadero found himself patting her back, the ready anger sizzling away inside him like some firecracker. "It's all over now. Just get yourself ready to ride and we'll cut across the range at its far corner from the ranch-house and we'll be long gone before they realise we've slipped out of their net."

Betsy wiped her nose on Buscadero's shirt cuff. She looked like some trail tramp, with her torn grey stuff skirt, bare legs and scuffed boots and the shirt several sized too big for her. It had been a long time since she'd last washed or combed her hair. It trailed down her back like brown rats' tails but he looked at her with a certain admiration. This girl had guts. She was a born survivor.

Then, the roan fed and watered with an extra handful of oats for he would well need the extra feed to carry two, they set off on the hazardous journey from the desert badland into the more fertile plain. Twice they saw small groups of men ranging the far slopes. Buscadero smiled thinly. This was his country. He could play hide and seek all day with such as these. But having Betsy with him stayed his hand. Best get her back to Jimmy the barber. Instinctively he knew that Jimmy would know what to do with the girl. Then, and only then would he put into operation the plan that until now had only been the glimmer of an idea. His lips drew back in a vicious snarl. It would be a joy as well as a duty to put paid to the Maddison name . . .

It was time he telegraphed to his good friend, Marshal Jack Calorhan. He might be just interested in Maddison for Buscadero's sharp eyes had noted something interesting. Those steers they'd seen at intervals were a mixed bunch with several brands, and one brand had stood out clearly. The old OXO brand from Tom Schneider's ranch more than two hundred miles away. A long way for beeves to stray . . .

★ ★ ★

Cal Emmett and his boys had returned past sundown. They'd been shocked to find the cook slumped dead in a pool of blood on Maddison's living-room floor and no sign of either him or his young brother Paul.

The men had spread out to look for them in the surrounding buildings and it was Cal himself who heard the faint knocking on the heavy wooden door of the underground storehouse where Paul crouched.

The boy had crawled up the wooden

steps and had knocked repeatedly for hours until he was exhausted from heat and the lack of water in the heavy foetid darkness. It had occurred to him fleetingly just how much Betsy Yates had suffered alone and in darkness with the dread of repeated rapes and beatings. But the thought was forgotten before it could register fully. Paul Maddison was too selfish to pity others. He was more worried about getting out himself than worrying about what condition his brother was in.

Cal Emmett shot the lock off the door and both Maddisons were carried to the ranch-house amidst much speculation about what had taken place.

Emmett listened to Joss K. Maddison's cursings for somehow it appeared to be his fault.

"It ain't our fault, boss," he protested. "They was your orders, boss. You said those there rustled beeves had to be delivered on the dot at the siding. As it was the train was early and we could hear its toot a long ways from where we gonna put 'em aboard. We was lucky it was old Jake and his crew or we would have missed the train altogether."

"Did you pay him like I said?"

"Why, yes, boss. He took the money for all them guards as well."

"Then where's the receipt?"

"He didn't give me none. There was no time. We got them steers aboard those cattle trucks and then it was skedaddle time."

"So they'll go straight through to Abilene. Did Jake say anything about Ventnor picking 'em up?"

"Yeh. The same procedure as last time. Money up front at the right time, like always."

Maddison grinned, despite the hurt shoulder.

"That's five hundred head to the good. You'll all get your bonuses come Saturday night."

"Now what about this feller, Buscadero, and the girl?"

Maddison's face changed. He looked at Cal Emmett and there was a knowing look in his eyes which Cal recognised.

"I want that bastard taking care of good," he said vindictively. "I don't give a shit about the girl. You can do with her what you will." He glance-around at the listening riders. "You can all share her . . . " There were grins and a licking of lips.

"How many of us do you want out there huntin' them up?"

"It shouldn't take more'n four of you. Young Paul's out of it with his injured foot and someone's gotta take care of Cookie. We'll haveta have us a buryin'."

"Then you'd better spell it out, boss. We've to shoot him on sight?"

"Yeh, shoot him down like the prairie wolf he is."

"And the girl?"

"As I said, do what you like with her. I don't want the bitch back! Take her up to the line camp and fasten her up. It's outta the way and as long as you remember to feed her she'll be entertainment for you boys on winter nights!"

The men drew lots as to who should stay behind and do the sweating. The ground was hard-packed and Cookie had to be sunk well down. The poor old sod deserved a decent burying even though he was a slapdash cook and heavy on the gutrot.

The chosen four left at sunrise then split to quarter the range and read for sign. It should be as easy as eating pumpkin pie to locate his tracks . . .

★ ★ ★

Buscadero and the silent girl watched the far distant horsemen. Buscadero laughed silently, Betsy watched him curiously.

"What's so funny?"

"Those fellers. Think they know this range. They're like babes in arms. They're sure in for a big shock!"

"Why, what are you dredging up for them?" He twisted round to look at her. This time she was riding behind him so that he could set a decent pace.

"I'm taking you to Jimmy and then I'm rustling up my good friend, Marshal Jack Calorhan, then with a bit of help, we'll gather up all the beeves on this here range and herd them in front of the ranch. I have a feeling that the result will be an embarrassment to Maddison. I don't think there will be many beeves with the Maddison brand on them. I think this is a clearing station for rustled stock."

"But how would he do that?"

"Simple. The railroad crosses his range in the far corner well away from any busy trail route. He's got some of the railroad crews on his payroll. The empty boxcars are being filled up before they reach the yards at Greenwater Spring. Easy done. The cattle inspector on the freight train just has to tell the rail boss in Greenwater Spring that he's picked up a special consignment of beeves for one of the big meat companies and he'll let 'em through and no questions asked. Maybe he's on the payroll too!"

"So that's why Maddison and his father moved in and hounded your father in the beginning, because the railroad went over part of your land and there was a natural stopping-place where it would be easy to herd hoofers aboard?"

"Now you've got the picture. Clever girl!"

"And will your plan work?"

"We'll make it work."

"I'm sure you will!" and he was certain that her arms had hugged him that little bit tighter.

★ ★ ★

Jimmy looked at them both, big-eyed.

"So you did it. I never thought you'd find her. I thought she was dead."

"I might as well have been and if it hadn't been for Buscadero here,

Maddison could have kept me hidden away as a sex slave forever, or as long as it took to tire of me."

"The dirty bastard! He took advantage of you?" Jimmy's staring eyes showed he could hardly believe the depravity of the man. "Just wait until Carrie hears about how you've been treated! She was sure you'd deliberately taken him away from her. She was the one who helped pass on those rumours about you and Susie."

"I should slap her down for Susie's sake," fumed Betsy. "What about me having a bath?"

Jimmy jumped.

"By God, it did occur to me when you first rolled in! In fact you both need baths. I suppose it will be ladies first, uh?" He grinned. "I think we can stretch the water for two baths."

"You can shave me while I'm waiting," Buscadero suggested, "and there's some extra dough to get her some respectable women's duds and something for the liveryman. I want

72

the roan currying and a set of new shoes fixing."

"Sure, I'll see to it for you."

"Good. Then after I've had a shave I'm going to the telegraph office."

Jimmy didn't ask why. He didn't want to be involved in the coming fight. He knew it was going to be messy and if young Edward Juantes didn't make out, he wanted to be on the winning side. Joss K. Maddison was a vindictive man. He'd seen some of Maddison's rough justice meted out by his men . . .

Buscadero felt better after a feed and his shave and better still after the long hot bath that loosened up legs stiffened by clamping themselves round the muscular stomach of the roan. He also perked up when he saw a clean Betsy dressed with feminine coyness in a blue sprigged dress with a low lace collar. Now don't go and get carried away, he chided himself. She's not the demure little innocent she appears right now. She's just as

73

alluring as the luscious Carrie but with less meat and more potato! He reminded himself sternly that permanent womenfolk meant excess baggage and he could do without the aggravation. Still . . . a woman to warm a man of nights, every night, might be worth the aggravation. Then he kicked himself hard on the shin and the pain drowned out other rising emotions. Buscadero had a reputation. He rode alone. His lifestyle wasn't that of a man with a woman breathing down his neck. No sir!

He sent his telegraph. Now all he had to do was wait. He saw Betsy walking into the haberdasher's and dodged out of her way. The fool girl was engrossed in spending some of her father's money. Well, let her. The poor kid deserved a shopping-spree.

Then a thought struck him between the eyes. What if she was in the family way through that bastard or Emmett or whoever else had mauled her about? He'd never had the courage to ask how many. He was surprised to find that what had happened didn't make the slightest difference and neither would the outcome whatever it was. She was still a gutsy young creature and dangerous to his peace of mind. Probably his liking for her was because she was the daughter of his old pal Davey and he felt a certain responsibility for her. But why he should when her father never did, he couldn't fathom. But there it was.

He rolled a cigarette and drew deeply and meditated. It was dangerous when you couldn't get a woman out of your mind. The answer was to find another.

He returned to the barber-shop. Jimmy was the only man he could trust in this backwater. He could probably recommend some woman other than luscious Carrie. He couldn't fancy her again, if she was the only whore left for a radius of fifty miles. Not after the way she shot at him with her little derringer. A man could only suffer so much. No, what he needed was a nice slim young thing, something like Betsy . . .

"Damn," he muttered out loud, "goldarn all women!" Jimmy heard his mutterings. He was just cleaning off his cut-throat razor while a little man lay back on the chair waiting to be dried off. Jimmy shook the razor at Buscadero.

"What you need, is the love of a good woman!"

"Depends what you're talking about. You mean good in bed, or one of these psalmsinging women who'd freeze the balls . . . " The man in the chair snickered. Jimmy grinned and then sighed.

"You action men are all the same. All you think about is fighting or floosying."

"Yeh, we're always ready for the quick draw either way. But you're wrong about one thing."

"And what's that?"

"We don't fight for no reason and

we set much store on feuding! We've got our pride."

Jimmy continued drying off his customer and then the little man paid up quickly and shot off, no doubt ready to tell the town Buscadero was back. Jimmy watched him go.

"You know who that was?"

"No, and I don't care."

"He's one of Maddison's yes men."

"A pity. I could have sent a message."

"What are you doing now?"

"Waiting for the marshal to show. If I know Jack, he'll be here on the next train."

He was right. Marshal Jack Calorhan stepped off the west-bound train two days later. He was a small man by western standards, blond going grey, a whiplash of a man just over five feet seven with a lived-in face and a pleasant smile for those he considered friends. He and Buscadero had first met way back in Kansas when they were both hunting Mighty Mick Fitzwilliams, the

Irish railroad foreman who'd embezzled fifty thousand dollars of railroad wages and the Missouri, Kansas and Texas Railroad Company bosses had drafted in both men to get on to the big Irishman's track.

A firm friendship had formed between them and on several occasions one or the other might call for help, and rarely had the call been in vain.

Buscadero was waiting, lounging in the shade of the station house, a half-smoked cigarette dangling, with wispy smoke making him screw up his eyes. He gave the impression of being carelessly curious about the passengers alighting at this stop.

Jack Calorhan saw him but gave no sign. He handed in his ticket and picked up the old carpetbag he toted everywhere with him, then he walked back to the box cars and supervised the slippery transfer of the temperamental chestnut gelding. Then patting him to soothe a ruffled temper, he led him out of the gathering crowd of hangers on and waiting relatives and walked the horse down the dirt road and into town. He hitched his horse in front of the Station Hotel and went inside and hired a room.

Buscadero waited outside. This was the usual procedure.

Buscadero followed leisurely behind, aware of watching eyes. Any of these town loafers could be in the pay of Joss K. Maddison. He lounged along Main Street and after two cigarettes casually entered the El Dorado saloon. It was dim and cool inside. He ordered a beer and drinking half of it at a near gulp, turned and hooked one elbow on the bar top and surveyed the entrance and the customers sitting at the rickety tables either talking or playing poker. The air was heavy with blue smoke and the stench of spilled beer and hard liquor caught at the throat.

It wasn't Buscadero's favourite kind of watering hole but it would serve. The little man who'd been shaved at the barber's shop nodded and sauntered over and put his beer down beside his.

"Howdy. You're the feller Jimmy said wanted a good woman." His eyes went up to the ceiling. "Is that what you're aimin' for? She's the best in town."

Buscadero laughed. "A bit too rich for the likes of me. Carrie looks good and she knows her worth. I'm not in the same league as guys like Maddison and his ilk."

"Between you and me and Carrie's bedpost, she's not been so popular in that quarter, nor any of the whores in town. He's gotta have something special out there on that lone ranch of his. Carrie's mighty upset about it. She was his main adam's rib and she don't like it none. When she's drunk she lets us all know what a skunk he is. Carrie's on the lookout for a bit of something fresh!" and he gave Buscadero an exaggerated wink. "How's about it, feller?"

"What's it to you? Are you her pimp?

Isn't she making enough money for you?"

The little man scowled.

"I was just being neighbourly. Thought you looked as if you needed a bit of fun . . . "

"Well, lay off, buster. I'm a big boy. I can make my own running, thank you very much!"

The little man shrugged, the breezy goodwill gone.

"Suit yourself. But remember, it pays to go along with the townsfolk and grease a few palms. Its mighty queer how Maddison finds out what going on and who's in town!"

Suddenly Buscadero whirled, the half-full pot of beer thrown in the little man's face.

"You think yourself mighty lucky I'm not in a trigger-happy mood today," and he grasped the goggle-eyed man's collar and twisted it until he was gasping and choking. Then he lifted him with ease several inches from floor and shook him like a rag doll. Then, with hardly flexed muscles he flung him back against the batwinged entrance and the little feller crashed through to sprawl in the dust in the road.

Buscadero followed and stood with legs apart and hands flexing near his gun butts. "Now you've got something extra to tell that boss of yours! Make the story good. Tell him, Buscadero's still in town and throwing his weight about!"

The man scrambled to his knees, blood flowing from a grazed forehead.

"He'll get you for this, feller, I'm warning you! The whole town knows what happened out there and he'll come gunning! He'll also get that girl he hid away . . . "

"What do you know about her?" and Buscadero made to lunge at the man, but the little feller was up and running down the alleyway at the side of the saloon. Buscadero didn't try to follow. He had an important appointment to keep.

Inside the saloon, the men were

waiting for the outcome. Some watched for further action while others went on with their games. Maddison's little shit-stirrer was univerally disliked by the honest citizens of Greenwater Spring.

The barman spat on the floor behind his counter and rubbed it into the floorboards with the toe of his boot.

"Serve the little arse-licker right. Here, have a beer on the house," and sent a beer flying down the long counter to stop in front of Buscadero. He rather prided himself on his calculated aim. He reckoned it was a gift. He was good with a shotgun too.

"Thanks, bud. Here's mud in your eye!" The barman studied the low-slung Colts. Their position and the way they were tied down had already alerted him and any drinkers present that this man would be useful in a quick draw depending whether you were on his side or facing him.

"You reckon to be using them guns in the near future?"

"Maybe," Buscadero took another

gulp. The barman kept his beer real cool.

"How about doing me a favour, feller and go and do your drinking somewheres else?"

Buscadero cocked a knowing eye.

"And why should I do that?"

"Because if I know anyone, that Billy Bones will be half way to Maddison's ranch by now and they'll be all thundering into town, the whole shebang of 'em baying for your blood!"

"Good. That's what I want 'em to do."

The barmen looked at him goggled-eyed. "What? You'd take on the goddamn lot of 'em? You must be loco."

Buscadero only smiled, and the barman went off to serve a short blond going-grey stranger, shaking his head. While his beer was being drawn, he missed the hint of an acknowledgment between the newcomer and the man dressed all in black.

5

MARSHALL Jack Calorhan accepted the beer and threw some coins down on the counter. He drank thirstily and then said to the watching barman,

"What was the ruckus out there?" The barman glanced at Buscadero.

"You wanna ask him. He's half of the ruckus," and moved away to serve a noisy customer who was fast becoming drunk.

Jack Calorhan moved closer with a casualness that would deceive anyone watching for suspicious moves.

"Just got into town," he said in a loud enough voice so that anyone interested wouldn't get earache by straining his lugs. "I'm a cattlebuyer from Kansas.' What was your bit of trouble?"

Buscadero shrugged. "Just a little snot threatening me. I put him in his place. No sweat."

"How about the entertainment in this neck of the woods?"

"Not bad if you like it rough."

Jack Calorhan nodded. "Any good poker schools?"

"They say the big guys come in at night and play for big stakes. What's your play?"

Jack Calorhan shrugged.

"Anything you can bet a ten-spot on."

"Then I advise you to lay low and make yourself ready for an all-night session, mister." The two men smiled at each other and at least one man present was listening with interest. There was a cattlebuyer in town with money to burn. Maddison would want to know on both counts . . .

Buscadero emptied his glass and prepared to leave.

"Must be off. Belly calls so I'm going to find some chow."

"Hmm, maybe I'll come with you." Calorhan nodded and drank off the rest of his beer. They walked out casually together, two new acquaintances looking for grub.

They slowly moved along the sidewalk. There didn't appear anyone very interested in them and so they came to the chink eating-house. It was only partially filled. They chose a table at the back and both sat with their backs towards the wall.

They waited until the Chinese proprietor flip-flopped to their table laden with two steaming plates of food piled high with grilled steaks, onions and fried potatoes. Their first hunger pangs assuaged, the marshal's keen blue eyes raked Buscadero's face.

"Well? What's this all about? What can I do?"

Buscadero leaned forward and said in a low voice,

"Rustlers." Jack Calorhan raised grey eyebrows. Buscadero went on, "You remember that outfit you traced back from Chicago to Abilene and wiped out, two . . . three years ago? You killed an old guy who purported to be the leader and several more hardarses. Well, I think I've found his son playing a similar game." Calorhan rasped his bristly chin.

"Yeh, I remember all right. It's not often anyone gets away from me. There was some unfinished business about that gang and it's always rankled. Are you sure about this?"

"I came on it by chance and the fact that this part of the world is my back yard, as it were. Joss K. Maddison is the man you want. It suddenly dawned on me how it had been worked, the freighted beeves and the way those men could disappear so easily."

"You don't say?" and Calorhan put his elbows on the table and forgot the food on his plate. "Tell me how it was done."

"Simple. I remembered the range where the railroad cut through my father's land in the most remote desert region. My old man didn't care. The railroad paid him a small fee for running through and as it was part of the badlands and no good for cropping, it was ignored and forgotten but useful for picking up a few dollars each year as rent. I remembered that there was one place where the ground was flat and hard. What better place to stop a train and load half a dozen empty box cars with beeves before they rolled into Abilene?"

"They would have to bribe the crew."

"Of course. The freight inspectors and the drivers and the attendants would be all in it and paid generously for every trip. Who would complain? Any passengers aboard would be told it was a scheduled stop if they were curious. The train driver would be given his orders on Company paper. That was how it was done then and how it is done now."

Calorhan took a forkful of potatoes and chewed while he gave it some thought.

"That would explain many things

that we couldn't figure way back in the old man's time. It would also explain how one of them got away. Just took off into the blue and turned up at his own ranch."

"Far enough away from Greenwater Spring for anyone asking curious questions. It was said his father died of a heart attack, so maybe the local doc was in it too. Incidentally the doc was bushwacked only weeks later." They stared at each other.

"Looks like young Maddison covered his tracks. So, what's your plan?"

"I came to Greenwater Spring to find a girl and give her a legacy left from her father, Davey Yates."

Jack Calorhan nodded slowly, a half-smile tickling his lips. "One of your more questionable friends. I've heard of him."

"He was a good pard. He never let me down though he was a wild man," Buscadero said defensively. "I've never hidden the fact that my gun was for sale to top dollar whatever side it was on. You know that."

"Yeh, I know that and I know you, feller. You wouldn't bullshit me. Now go on, I take it Yates has kicked his chips?"

"Bushwacked. I promised to look up his girl and found her missing and rumour had it she was with Maddison. I went looking for her and on the way picked up the surprising signs that the ranch was running other people's stock but surprisingly little of Maddison's own brand. I also recognised some of the brands that should not have been in these parts. I know some of the owners of those brands and there's no way those cows could have strayed or been sold down the track. They had to be rustled. They were also slowly working their way over to the railroad and then it struck me about the natural stopping-point. I made a few discreet enquiries and found that unscheduled stops did occur down the line and it's possible another is, due. Now you and I could organise another stop . . . "

"And . . . ?"

"There could be shootists aboard and a few deputies."

"But we'd have to wait for them to play the right game."

"Not necessarily so. You could take on Maddison tonight. They say he's a crazy gambler when he starts. Plays for real big stakes and I know when he hears you're in town he's going to be there to challenge you to the big stuff. He doesn't get many chances of playing the big money boys. He's bound to take the bait."

"And then?"

"You keep him playing all night. Cal Emmett will also be by his side watching no one takes a peep over his shoulder."

"Then what?"

"You know the sheriff of this burg. He and I and some of his deputies will nudge up the herd so that it's waiting down by the railtrack."

"At about five in the morning when his morale is at its lowest, a rumour will start that rustled cows are running over the railtrack. He'll be losing . . . "

"How do you know that? He might be a better player than I am, especially when big money is at stake."

Buscadero gave a short laugh. "Don't try the funnies with me, Marshal. I know you spent ten years as a riverboat gambler before you saw the light! You know more sleight of hand tricks than a pickpocket in a nudist colony!"

Marshal Jack Calorhan laughed with amusement.

"You've got gall, Buscadero. It's a long time since I cheated to get justice done, but, thinking about it, I must say I'm tempted. I wonder just how deep his pocket is, and what's the ethics about the winnings?" They both laughed together and several customers wondered what the joke was that tickled the two strangers.

"As far as I'm concerned," Buscadero muttered softly, "your winnings are your own and no questions asked."

The marshal scraped his plate clean

with a piece of bread, mopping up the onion gravy.

"You're on. After all, we'd be cleaning up a nest of jackals in the process. What happened to the girl?"

"I brought her back to Greenwater Spring. In fact, she's coming in here now," and they both turned to watch the door and the marshal gave a low whistle.

"Now I can understand your interest in all this!"

Buscadero gave him an irritated glance. The old fool, knew his views on women. All right in the sack for a night's gymnastics but as a permanent weight round is neck . . . no way! This girl was a responsibility, no more, no less . . .

"Aw, shucks, Marshal, you know me better than that!"

"You're a man, ain't uh? Don't be a sap! You're old enough to settle down, boy." He was smiling and talking out the side of his mouth as he nodded to the girl who was smiling at them both. She was laden down with rough-wrapped parcels. Looking flushed and excited she sat down with a pleased sigh.

"I'm worn out with deciding what to buy! I've never had such a lot of money to spend, Buscadero. It's a lovely feeling." He sat forward, ready to ask her if she'd blown the lot when her eyes met the marshal's. "I don't think we've been introduced. Are you a friend of Buscadero's?"

The marshal hitched himself in his chair and coughed. The question had been asked in a high innocent voice. He looked around before answering and encountered the grin on Buscadero's face. The girl put him in a jam.

"Well, now . . . breakfast acquaintances, you might say," he drawled and kicked out at Buscadero under the table. "May we order something for you, Miss . . . er . . . Miss?"

"Now that would be sure kind of you, Mr . . . er, I don't know your name."

"That's because we never told you," Buscadero butted in, a bit nettled at the way Calorhan was taking over. "Let me introduce you, Jack Calorhan . . . Betsy Yates, daughter of Davey . . . "

"He was a good man was Davey," Calorhan said smoothly and Buscadero gawked at him. The old devil . . . what was his game?

"So you knew my father too?" Betsy said eagerly and after the Chinaman came and took her order, "You knew him well?"

"Well, now, not too well. Saw his picture. He was quite famous back where I come from."

Buscadero smiled as he lowered his head to sup coffee. The marshal was responsible for putting away several of Davey's earlier pards before he and Buscadero met. Davey had had a chequered career before he'd started the bounty-hunting game and turned half-way respectable.

"So he was famous? I didn't know that." She turned to Buscadero and frowned. "You didn't tell me he was in the newspapers."

"Newspapers?" For a moment Buscadero was at a loss. He'd reckoned the marshal had seen a wanted poster of a much younger Davey. "Oh, ah . . . yes, of course. Forgot about that. Something about dodging a gang of rustlers, wasn't it, Jack?" and Buscadero's grin dared the marshal to tell the truth.

"Something like that, feller. I forget the details," Calorhan answered easily and then turned again to the girl. "What are you thinking of doing now, Miss?"

Betsy looked at Buscadero and then down at her plate.

"I don't know, it's up to Buscadero. He's looking after me now, Mr Calorhan."

The marshal raised his expressive eyebrows. "Oh? I wasn't aware of the exact situation or maybe I was being misled."

The girl looked at them both

97

and laughed. "Oh, there's nothing to mislead anyone about, Mr Calorhan. Dad left me in Buscadero's charge, and by the way he's looked after me until now, we'll probably get married!"

Buscadero coughed and half a cup of coffee sprayed the table. Jesus, Joseph and Mary! What the hell had he walked into?

Calorhan thumped him hard on the back and he was laughing like a drain.

"She's some woman, this girl of yours," he chortled, "knows her own mind. I've never had a woman propose to me before. You should be flattered!"

Betsy looked from one to the other with a puzzled look on her pretty face.

"I don't know what all the commotion's about but what we did the other night, Buscadero made me expect to be marrying him. Isn't that right?"

"Betsy, whatever happened between us is private business, not to be talked over a breakfast table."

"But you said . . . "

"I know what I said, now, please, Betsy, just shut up. Jack and I have some very important business to discuss."

She looked sulky. "I'm sorry. I suppose I shouldn't have come but I wanted to show you what I'd bought . . . "

"Later. Now if you've finished your breakfast?"

"But aren't you going to escort me to the hotel?"

Buscadero sighed. Women were all the alike. They had one-track minds.

"I said later, Betsy." She stood up sharply, her chair rocking dangerously.

"All right then, I'm going and I don't care if I never see you again!" and with that she gathered up her parcels and flounced away out of the restaurant.

Buscadero wiped sweat from his brow.

"Hell! I think I've got trouble." Calorhan shook his head and drew his lips together in a mock tut tut.

"That comes of playing around with amateurs. Best stick to the professionals. There's no back-lash. They know their place!"

"Aw, hell, shut your face!"

6

JACK CALORHAN was dressed for the part. He prided himself on his prowess at the card table. Although he hadn't stressed the point with Buscadero, shuffled and manipulated the cards every day of his life. Being a marshal back in Kansas didn't cramp his style. He never knew when his old skills would be useful. This was one of the times come up out of the blue. He had to admit to himself that he was looking forward to meeting Joss K. Maddison over the baize. There were different ways of trouncing a feller as well as shooting him up.

He looked at his reflection in his hotel mirror. He saw a tautly slim man in healthy middle age . . . he rarely dwelt on the fact that he wouldn't see fifty-five again. But the reason he was still alive was his dexterity in everything he did, whether shooting to kill, or playing cards for a gold cow, or keeping his mind alert to what was going on around him when enjoying a woman, especially when said woman had a man of her own . . .

He wore a well cut black jacket and tight pants with a frilled white shirt, all remains from his days on the river-boats. The lucky black jacket hid a few surprises. Along with a knife and a small derringer there were pockets to palm cards. He felt comfortable in it and confident. He tied a thin bootlace tie and set a tall black stetson firmly at an angle on his head. Black showed up the grey-blond hair, making it more blond than grey. He was pleased with his appearance. He wasn't only out to impress Maddison but any likely woman in the establishment. It always paid to have some woman rooting for him, if things happened to go wrong. In his experience nothing was one hundred per cent. One had to make allowances for Lady Luck to do her damnedest.

He smiled at his reflection. Already the adrenalin was flowing. He picked up the cards he'd been using earlier and riffled the pack and was satisfied. His hands had lost none of their earlier skill. He could always go back to the river-boats if he became sick of adminstering the law.

He made sure his law badge was still hidden. He'd not used it since coming to Greenwater Spring. He was living incognito. No need to alert anyone but the local sheriff about who was in town.

He thought of Sheriff Hank Stoner and wondered again if he was a wild card. He'd been none too pleased when he'd introduced himself and showed him his credentials. Took it hard that he hadn't introduced himself as soon as he hit town. He'd been dubious about rounding up his deputies for a night ride out to Maddison's ranch. He'd hummed and ha-ed and dredged up excuses why they shouldn't raid the most powerful rancher's range. He'd sat up with a jerk when he was told that some of Calorhan's own deputies were coming running. That they'd be on the train due at dawn which would stop at the cutting on Maddison's range.

Calorhan knew that if the news was leaked, then Sheriff Hank Stoner was going to be in big trouble.

He hoped Buscadero knew what he was doing or he, Calorhan, would be in big trouble.

He checked his wallet. It wouldn't do to be short of the ready. He also had notes from his bank. Over the years Calorhan had aquired quite a build-up of cash and stock for his old age. He didn't enforce the law for the money, he did it to right many wrongs he'd seen over the years. He slipped the wallet inside a deep pocket and was pleased to see that none of his pockets bulged. The tailor who'd made that jacket had charged him the earth for it, but the little Jew had been a genius. He'd made the money many times over since those days.

At last it was time to go. He checked his timepiece, a parting gift from his father which he only used on social occasions and times like this. It helped to overawe the opposition. It showed his adversaries he was no tow-rag.

They were waiting for him when he arrived at the El Dorado. Fleetingly he wondered whether tonight would bring him a pot of gold. He knew Buscadero would keep his word. Whatever he won tonight would be his own. Also he wondered just how Buscadero was doing. They would be well on their way. The cattle left on the range wouldn't be hard to round up. All the picked deputies were experienced cowhands. The muscles of his face stretched involuntarily as he saw Maddison waiting flanked by his ramrod and another big ugly-looking fellow. His smile was wide. It tickled his sense of humour to know that Maddison who was still suffering from a wound in the shoulder should think him so important as to come on the off-chance to play a high-rolling gambler.

Maddison was chewing a cigar nervously. The tension in the man showed clearly. Good. Calorhan liked his opponents stretched like fencing wire.

He paused for effect in the doorway of the El Dorado. Calorhan had much of the showman about him. A magnificently built woman in black satin and lace swanned towards him, hand outstretched, a smile on her lips which did not quite reach her eyes.

"Welcome to the El Dorado. We've all been waiting impatiently for you to show," and her glance took in all the men grouped round the round green baize table.

Calorhan grinned and took her hand and kissed it as if she was the governor's lady. Incredibly she blushed. He could have laughed.

"Dear lady, if I'd known of your impatience I should have made your acquaintance much earlier. What about sharing a bottle of your finest champagne?" The interest in the blue eyes deepened. He watched the tell-tale lift of her bosom. Women's chests were always a giveaway, specially belters like hers.

Her eyes fluttered and her black curls cascaded prettily down and over ample shoulders mingling with the froth of lace that scarcely hid her charms. She had the hips of a natural mother and a tightly laced waist which must be a bit of a trial but looked good, he assessed rapidly.

She escorted him like British royalty, to be introduced to Maddison while waving an imperious arm and mouthed the words best champagne to the gawking barman.

Maddison made it clear that Cal Emmett would remain behind him. The plug-ugly was Lars Zinnerman and he proved a restless bastard, moving backwards and forwards and wafting his stink to such an extent that Calorhan wondered whether it was deliberate to break his concentration. But Calorhan had played poker in many low dives. If he hadn't known better he would have said his ma had been a first-class skunk. He concentrated with savoir-faire and the only time his mind wasn't on his cards and what was going on around him was when Carrie Smithers filled his champagne glass. He didn't think she would slip him a mickey finn in the glass. Somehow he didn't think it her style. But Maddison owned the El Dorado. Maybe someone else like the barman might slip something in the bottle. Carrie Smithers might just be an innocent dupe, though he doubted it. It paid not to trust anybody.

He didn't drink as much as it was supposed. The frilled shirt had a secret of its own. It was possible to tip the wineglass fast and perhaps a tablespoon of wine would disappear into a flat funnelled phial that didn't show beneath the ruffles. It had served him well in the past. The only snag was calculating just how much he'd tipped. The phial held perhaps two glasses. It meant he had to leave the room at certain intervals to visit the outside privy and empty the contraption. There was no danger when he had one of his own stooges present to watch for interference of cards. This time he had no trusted watcher looking after his interests. But he'd come prepared. In one of his capacious pockets he carried several packs of new cards with the seals as far as could be seen unbroken . . .

He allowed Maddison to win the first five thousand in the kitty. It settled Maddison down and gave him a false sense of ease. The crowd drew closer as Maddison's bid grew higher and higher. His excitement was shown in how many cigars he mangled. He had the glazed look of the addicted gambler.

At first Calorhan thought maybe Maddison and his gang must be doing badly and Maddison was supplementing the rustling take with high-rolling gambling but Cal Emmett didn't act as if he was a sleeping partner allowing the boss to use his stake. He had the air of a man watching the play with only detached interest and this was more so when Calorhan decided to try his luck. He watched both men for their reactions. Maddison was furious. He was a bad loser and his hands shook badly when they picked up the next hand. Emmett had smiled as if to say, serve you bloody well right, with no indication that it was partly his money Calorhan had won. So, maybe Maddison was gambling away his own cut in the proceeds as they went along? Maybe Maddison wasn't as rich and powerful as the local townspeople estimated?

Calorhan began a campaign of losing two and winning one, and the one he won was spun out until it was quite a big take. The word had gone the rounds that there was a big game going on and men from the other saloons were filtering in. The place became jam-packed and for once the good-time girls were being ignored.

Carrie came to sit beside Calorhan. He could smell her warm flesh and the heavy cheap scent she'd doused herself in. She'd be quite something in bed, he opined, and found it just a little harder to concentrate. He grinned. He was proof against the plug-ugly's stink but Carrie's warm scent was reaching parts that the stink couldn't. He glanced at her.

"Get me a beef sandwich and a cup of coffee, lover," and his eyes caught and held hers and somehow sent out a message. She looked at him, sensing his interest.

"With pleasure," and she thrust out her bosoms and Calorhan was sure the coffee and food wouldn't be treated, then his mind went back to the job in hand. There were fifteen thousand dollars on the table and until now it was shifting from one side to the other and rising. He played the next hand and jacked the pot up another hundred spot. The crowd gasped. It was even getting a bit rich for Maddison who sweated profusely and kept pulling out a red handkerchief and mopping his brow.

Then, Carrie returned with the sandwiches and coffee. There was a lull while Maddison himself went to the privy. Calorhan ate and drank and looked at Carrie.

"Can I trust you to watch him when I go for a leak?" She nodded.

"Yes. You'll come to me after this is over?" she whispered quickly before Maddison returned.

"Of course." He smiled. "A victor needs the spoils of victory."

Suddenly she was alert, too alert.

"How do you know you're going to be the victor?"

He shrugged careless shoulders. "Any man who plays for big stakes expects to win. If he didn't, he'd be beaten before he starts."

She nodded as if satisfied with his answer. She leaned forward. "Be careful. No man wins big money from Joss. He calls the shots, you know."

"I guessed it, ma'am. I'm no greenhorn at this game." He smiled at her and stood up as Maddison came back into the room. He looked smug and pleased with himself. Calorhan looked round quickly for his two henchmen. The plug-ugly was missing.

He walked to the back door, nodding pleasantly to Maddison and stepped outside into the yard. All was in darkness but a tingle up his spine told him he wasn't alone. Out there was someone holding his breath and waiting!

He moved a few steps and decided he wouldn't enter the stinking privy to do what he had to do. Quickly feeling for the phial he tipped it and the faint glug of wasted champagne came to his ears. He pissed as it emptied to drown the suspicious sound that might alert the listener to the little subterfuge.

Then he recognized the smell. Lars Zinnerman was crouched close by. Unless he was to be cold-cocked it was time for a ground-hog case

. . . the first punch in a rough-house. He took a swing just as the plug-ugly's foetid breath threatened to choke him. It was a powerhouse drive and caught the man midway between jaw and chest. Calorhan could feel the adam's apple give as the man was flung back up against the privy door. He heard the body fall in the darkness. It had been a lucky swing. Once in a bearhug with a man of Zinnerman's size and the slighter Calorhan would have had his ribs crushed in.

His knuckles stung. Calorhan resisted the urge to blow on them and tuck them under his arm. He stepped inside the door and made his way leisurely to the green baize table and sat down. He caught the look of amazement on Maddison's face. He smiled.

"It's coming up to storm outside," he vouchsafed pleasantly. Maddison's attention was drawn to the bruised red knuckles showing a trickle of blood.

"You've hurt yourself out there?"

Calorhan looked at his hand.

"It was nothing. It's dark out there. I caught it against something when I was looking for the privy. Now where were we? Oh, I know, that last trick was mine. What do you say to a new pack of cards? It just so happens I've got a new unopened pack." He smiled at Maddison and then at those watching. "All right?" and put the new pack in the middle of the table. "Would you like to open them and deal, Mr Maddison?"

Maddison looked angry and a little suspicious but did as requested. He could hardly do otherwise. He had as many enemies as friends standing watching him play. Inwardly he fumed. Whatever happened tonight, he was going to get this smart-arse little man. For one thing he didn't like the way his old flame Carrie Smithers was arse-licking him. He'd ignored Carrie for months, ever since he'd made off with Betsy Yates, the young girl who'd got under his skin by defying him. If she'd come to him peaceable he would never have put the bitch through the humiliations he had. But her contempt of him had sent him loco. Now, he was ready to take Carrie back. She should be proud and willing to take up where he'd left off. But the stupid cow was being uppity. Jeepers creepers! what store some of these whores put on themselves! She'd be thinking of marriage next with some poor sod and she going on forty if she was a day!

If this stranger did what no man had ever done and lived to tell the tale, then his best whore might take her hook and catch him in the first flush of his success. So there was another reason why this bastard wouldn't be allowed to leave Greenwater Spring. If the worst happened, he would give Carrie Smithers a short sharp lesson she would never forget. What had happened to Betsy Yates would be nothing compared to what he would do to that seasoned hard bitch . . .

His fingers trembled as he riffled the new deck of cards. His imagination was running away with him and he was tiring. The strain was telling on him. He decided on the highest stakes he'd ever played with. He leaned forward.

"What about upping the ante?"

"How much?"

"A thousand a throw?"

Calorhan didn't hesitate.

"Why not?" he answered easily. "I take it you'll take a bankers draft?"

"Of course. I know you're a man of integrity."

"Thank you," and Calorhan studied his new cards. It was just as well, he'd brought out that particular pack of cards . . .

The crowd gasped at the stakes. There was enough they calculated on the table to make the townsfolk wealthy, the whole damn lot of them. Men watched, who would talk of this session for the rest of their lives when poker was mentioned.

"More champagne?" Carrie Smithers' eyes were shining. Calorhan wondered whether it was for him she was rooting,

117

or some skilfully conveyed instruction from her boss.

"Why not? I feel lucky. How about some more for yourself?" Carrie nodded and poured wine into her own glass first and then sipped, nodding slightly. Calorhan smiled. It was her way of saying the wine was not doctored.

He drank and the wine cleared his throat of stale food and air tainted with smoke. It sharpened his wits and heightened his awareness. Glancing at his watch he saw that most of the night had ticked away. It would soon be dawn and soon a messenger would be arriving to put the fear of hell up Maddison and scare him shitless. He stretched and looked at Maddison.

"Why not one last grand slam throw? I'm putting the ante up to five thousand. How about it?" Maddison's eyes bugged and his throat worked. "I'm getting bored. After all, it's only money. I also want my bed," and he looked with a smile at Carrie, making sure that Maddison saw the byplay.

Maddison was furious.

"Five thousand? Are you mad?"

"Not from where I sit, Mr Maddison. Of course if you're not used to big-league playing . . . " Maddison choked on the whisky he was drinking. "The devil take you! I've never gone past my limit yet! Look, between us, we've got more than fifty thousand on the table and by the looks of it, you've got the biggest share. I'll stake all I've got to all of yours on one last hand!" Emmett tugged at his arms but Maddison thrust him away furiously. "What about it?"

"Yes, but with the added stake of five thousand each!"

Maddison stared and gulped.

"You're not being serious?"

"Why not? As I said, it's only money."

"But . . . " Then Maddison pulled himself together. He remembered what he'd sworn to do with Calorhan. The man would never leave Greenwater Spring alive . . .

"You're on. We'll cut a new pack

119

of cards and this time they'll be my cards," and Maddison gave Calorhan a fish-eyed look that said for that money, he wouldn't trust his own mother.

"Very well," and while they waited for a new pack, Maddison bit another cigar to chew.

Suddenly there was a commotion and the back door opened with a crash and a couple of swampers dragged in the unconscious Lars Zinnerman and left him lying on the floor.

"Hey, Maddison," one of them shouted with malicious jocularity, "we found one of your nursemaids laid out cold. The man who did this packs a wollop!" and Maddison's nostrils pinched as he looked down at Calorhan's bruised hand.

"Yeh, I imagine he would," he said slowly and looked into Calorhan's eyes. Calorhan started a tattoo on the table even though the movement sent splinters of pain up his arm. He grinned.

"I thought I'd hit a block of wood,

on the other hand, I think I did. What do you think, Maddison?" Maddison spat on the floor. It would be a pleasure to sick his men on to this little smart-arse bastard. It might take three to do a good job . . .

Maddison gave the new deck to Calorhan to unwrap and inspect. He'd only just started on the ritual when a stranger smelling of fresh horse-sweat carved a passage through the crowds to reach Maddison's side amidst grumbles from watching men who'd had ribs punched by sharp elbows and toes trodden on by uncaring feet. The man bent low and whispered into Maddison's ear and Calorhan's mouth twitched. This was the man he'd been waiting for, the man who was bringing the news about the gathering of beeves at his private rail station.

He watched Maddison look up sharply, his face draining white.

"What the hell do you mean?" he said in a loud whisper. He couldn't hide his agitation and Calorhan would have bet his bowels were acting like a dry waddy after the rains came flooding down. Any minute now there would be an overflow . . . He would be crapping in his mukluk as his friends up Alaska would have put it.

Then Maddison was swearing and he looked wildly around at sychophants and enemies alike and then his hot eyes rested on Calorhan who was sitting back at ease drinking a little champagne.

"You!" he mouthed and pointed a forceful finger in the marshal's face. "You're mixed up in this somehow, or why . . . " Then looking with hot eyes at the pile of bills, he breathed deeply to control his fury and said swiftly, "I'm taking my dough . . . "

As if by magic the snub-nosed little derringer was aimed directly at Maddison's forehead.

"Not before you win it fair and square, buster! The deal's still on." There was silence all around the room. No one stirred. Maddison swallowed and let his hands fall flat on the table.

"Look, this is no time to gamble. I've got rustlers raiding my stock. Let's call it quits. You take your pile and I'll take mine."

"No!" The refusal came as sharp as a whiplash. "I don't play that way, mister, especially when you've just accused me of being in on whatever's troubling you. The deal stays unless you want to lose by default."

"Why you . . . " Maddison choked with rage. "Very well, deal and be damned!"

Calorhan smiled. This was what he was waiting for. He'd even got the deal. Now was the time to prove his own skill . . .

Maddison stared down at the straight flush and swore, then flung down his own cards.

"Curse you, Calorhan! But there'll be another time!" and he swung away from the table. His nod was unseen by most of the onlookers but Calorhan was looking for such a sign. He was tossing money into his hat when Cal Emmett suddenly swung round, his gun arching for a killing shot. The crowd responded by shouts and yells and in the background a woman screamed. There was a pushing and shoving and above the din, Calorhan heard Maddison roar, "Get him!"

Two blasts merged simultaneously and Calorhan still sitting at the table held his smoking pocket gun in one hand and a clutch of bills in the other. The watching crowd saw Cal Emmett keel over and slowly sink to the floor, a small round hole which trickled blood appearing between the eyes. His eyes steely as he looked the crowd over.

"Anyone else with a grudge?" and as no one answered, he calmly scooped up the rest of his winnings and dropped them into his hat. Then his eyes caught Carrie standing back against the bar. "Hey! Carrie, be a good girl and look after this for me? I've got a pressing engagement." She stared at him fascinated. This was a cool deadly bastard . . .

"When will you be back?"

"Oh, I'll be back." He smiled and looked at the eye-popping cleavage. "Too true, I'll be back and not just because of the cash!" He laughed and chucked her under the chin. "Take good care of that, sweetheart. It means life or death to you!"

She watched him go with purposeful strides to the door. He paused and gave her a little wave. She shivered. God help her if she made off with his cash . . .

7

THE round-up was taking time, more than Buscadero calculated. It seemed that Maddison had pruned his range for beeves and the rest had not yet gathered themselves into one main herd. Small numbers had instinctively grouped together and various brands had clung together through familiarity. But the evidence was damning. The rustled cattle were inside a hastily strung fence and could no way have been strays by chance. The fenced area took in the whole length of the railroad that cut into an isolated corner of Maddison's land.

Buscadero set his mouth grimly. This land had changed since his boyhood days when his father ran the range freely with a few beeves and the fertile land divided into fields. Now the fields were no longer farmed and were once again gone back to grass. He shook his head to clear it oblong ago memories best left forgotten. He cracked his whip and the cows he'd rounded up lumbered forward to join a larger herd, their calves bawling after them.

There was a huge dust blow covering the night sky. The air stank with the smell of the round-up. It was choking, gruelling work that taxed both man and beast. It was dangerously near dawn and the rail engine pulling the stock-cars would be steaming to the stopping point in less than two hours. He hoped fervently his plan would work.

But gradually everything was taking shape. Most of the beeves were settling down in the great pen Maddison had caused to be fashioned. The newcomers acted up a little but soon settled with the earlier arrivals.

The deputies in charge of the herd rode slowly around the perimeter, humming softly to soothe the beasts. A stampede would tear down the single strand of wire and allowing for many casualties, the bulk of the herd would be unstoppable. No one who'd sweated his life's blood to get the herd together wanted to see the plan fail.

If Maddison reacted in the way he should, he should come lickety-spit with his riders to take on the rustlers who'd had the nerve to come in his absence, and take advantage of the train passing through. Some bastard amongst them talking too much in his cups or for money, and broadcasting his little secret. He would come with guns blazing. No one should be left alive . . . But he wouldn't be reckoning on a new crew on board the train or the hidden State marshal and his deputies.

They heard the thundering of hooves long before the riders hove into view. Maddison was past caution. This was his land. He had a right to ride across it in any manner he pleased. They came guns blazing and the only thing wrong was that there was no return fire. The preliminary shots started the herd pushing and shoving, cows calling for lost calves and calves bawling for absent mothers while bad-tempered steers played lockhorns with growing savagery through sheer frustration.

The men pulled up and divided, riding cautiously in two's around the perimeter. Maddison had recruited extra men in town tempted by the pay which was over the odds.

"Shit!" he roared. "What the hell's going on? Some goddamn sonofabitch reported rustlers. Where the hell are they?"

A little wizened man on horseback rode forward. He knew exactly what he'd been told to say. Now he repeated the words verbatim.

"There's a stock train due here at five o'clock, Mr Maddison. Emmett said we had to have a herd ready. We did what you said, boss. There's close on six hundred barring the calves. We had to run 'em all to get the beeves together. They're all set, Mr Maddison, Sir."

Maddison scratched his head and then replaced his hat.

"What the hell are you talking about? I didn't order another round-up!"

The little man blinked. "It was Mr Emmett himself, Sir, who passed on the word . . . "

"But Emmett was with me tonight." He looked at the little man with suspicion. "I don't know you . . . "

The little man smiled. "No, Mr Maddison. Mr Emmett just took me on. Told me and the other fellers a few days ago. I been up on line camp rounding up strays."

Maddison scowled. "Sounds like a double-cross. Did he tell you to keep mum?"

"Well, now you mention it, boss, he was a bit . . . "

"A bit what?"

"Why, kind of furtive, Sir. I never dreamed . . . "

"Huh! I always thought Emmett would come up with something some day. Well, let me tell you, feller,

Emmett got his tonight."

The little man gawped.

"You don't say! Now what do we do, Sir?"

Maddison laughed. "Carry on with the plan. If Emmett got himself a fiddle going, I might as well cash in. Get round the fellers and tell 'em, the moment the train's in sight to start funnelling the herd to the loading gates."

"Yes Sir!" and the little man rode off into the darkness.

Maddison watched him go. So Emmett had shit in his nest after all. He thought bitterly about young Paul. If he'd been anything like a brother, the young bugger would have been on the lookout for trouble. He was the one who frequented the bunkhouse to play cards with the boys. He should have been listening in for trouble. He wondered how many more of the men were in Emmett's scheme. He'd get rid of the lot of them when this little bit of business was cleaned up, and he wouldn't be paying wages and telling them to git. He knew just the man to waste them. He pondered about Paul and what to do about him. He was his brother, and yet . . . The little bastard was lazy and he cost money to keep sweet, and then some time he'd be wanting half . . . Maybe he'd be better off including him in the deal he'd make with Two-gun Luke Wade . . .

★ ★ ★

Buscadero was cramped and uncomfortable. The wind was cold and he'd been hiding on the ridge ever since Maddison and his riders had come storming in. The little man, Mo Morris, had come crawling to him, grinning all over his mutton chops.

"He swallowed it, Mr Buscadero, hook, line and sinker. He's going ahead with the shipment. Can't resist talking advantage of the train stopping."

"He swallowed it about Emmett?"

"Yeh, I got the impression he'd been

expecting Emmett to come up with some double-cross. He was mad but not very surprised."

"Good. Now all we have to do is wait and get them all in the crossfire and caught red-handed. I'd like to see the bastard's face when he realises the train's bristling with railroad cops!"

Dawn was already breaking. Streaks of orange and pink gave temporary colour to far-away mountains and nearer escarpments. There were still blue-black shadows under rock bluffs. It was still hard to discern what was happening.

Buscadero crawled free and bellied near the area of struggling cows. Far away shots were being fired. Buscadero smiled grimly and caught sight of his man on his left. He waved. It was a signal to the man to draw closer and pass the word to the other deputies. As soon as the coming train came to a standstill and the first beeves were taken aboard, it would be the time to strike.

Then came the long-drawn-out whistle of the oncoming train. Nerves tightened and guns were checked. Buscadero went back to where his mount was tethered. Soon it would be time to show that bastard Maddison the trap that had been set.

Cautiously the deputies moved in to follow the circle of milling cows, the noise of restive animals a cacophony of sound so loud a man would have to shout his loudest to be heard, and yet in amongst the deafening sound could be heard the short sharp explosions of guns fired to manoeuvre the beeves into the wide funnel-like aperture needed to load them into the boxcars.

The slowing train and the jet of black smoke panicked the animals nearest the line. There were shouts and whips cracked and horses neighed and there was much cursing until some kind of control was created.

"Get those bloody doors opened and the ramps fixed, goddamn you!" bawled Maddison to the guards who could be seen peering from the last boxcar.

Suddenly he felt a strange tingling in his spine. This wasn't the usual train that passed through on its three-times-a-week run to Abilene. Where were the bloody passengers and the mail car? This engine was pulling eight cars only. He glanced at the sweating men straining to get the cows aboard, neither they nor those concentrating on separating cows from calves had noticed anything wrong. He could see a number of men aboard the train working at opening up the cattle-wagons but . . .

His breath caught in a choking wheeze as the stock-car ramps were laid down and suddenly there were men with rifles everywhere and the men in the forefront already at the side of the track controlling the input of the beeves were going down in the first blast of fire.

In a crystal-clear flash he knew he and his men were in a trap. Three-quarters of the men with him were bunched together, their minds on moving steers. None had any warning. It was like mowing down a set of dummies. Some fell under the hooves of frenzied beasts while others raked their horses and turned to escape the hail of bullets only to run smack into the moving column of steers. Maddison's mind clicked and his decision to leave came swiftly. That was why he'd become a leader. No messing. No trying to be a hero. Yet he would have liked a shot at the man in black and that bastard, Calorhan, who'd played him for a sucker.

Then incredibly he found himself outmanoeuvred. There was an outer flank of horsemen. They must have ridden up behind them. Panic now seized Maddison and cold sweat trickled down his forehead stinging his eyes. To get beyond the danger, he must charge through a hail of bullets from a menacing stand of horsemen. He watched two of his men with the same idea charge the waiting line and saw them both shot out of the saddle. He saw Buscadero handle his guns and a third and fourth man go down. It passed fleetingly through his mind they were like rathunters standing round a hayrick waiting for the rodents to come out and then deliberately waiting until they had a bead on them before firing. They were so many rats . . .

Then hope returned. He saw a horse running free, its saddle red with blood and it was galloping towards him, wild of eye and foaming at the mouth. It was his only chance. As it galloped by he leaned forward and grabbed its flying rein. He was jerked out of his own saddle and the two horses galloped away side by side dragging him between them. He hauled clear, but he was bruised and he was sure he'd busted at least one rib.

He grinned mirthlessly. A busted rib was nothing for the chance of going free! He hung on grimly and it was fortunate his own gelding was pulling to the left and away from the gun-crazed steers and up a steep incline. His body weight slowly took the steam out of both horses and slowly they came to rest with heads hanging and foam-lathered necks. He was trembling. He could hardly believe his luck. He allowed the second horse to wander off while he struggled to regain his saddle. For a long while he stayed still in the saddle, his head hanging while he breathed deeply to ease his aching arms. Then he put spur to still heaving ribs and rode off at an angle away from the press of animals and well to the rear of the still intermittent gunfire.

His next stop would be the ranch. He would pick up what was in the safe and leave the rest for young Paul. They had nothing on the boy. He was pig-sick of having him hanging round his neck like the devil's load. He wanted out. The boy was old enough to stand or fall on his own merits. Maddison had no conscience about leaving him. His own folks had left them both for years until he, Joss, had been useful to his father as second in command in the ranch he'd hounded the Mexican farmer for whom he'd subsequently killed along with his wife. No, young Paul would have more than ever he had to start. And he hadn't been saddled with a young brother . . . To hell with the ranch!

Both horse and man were at their lowest ebb. No matter how he willed himself, Maddison hadn't the strength to ride at full stretch. He also knew that pushing the horse between his legs would kill the brute. He didn't want that. The beast could run in the corral and he would take the dappled grey when he finally rode away from his ranch. He was conscious of a pang. He'd improved it immensely from the time he took it over from his father. The old man had only used the once prosperous farmstead to run other people's cattle. Joss had fenced more land, built corrals and planted windbreaks in the years since his father died. He wouldn't have believed the resentment he was now feeling at the thought of leaving it all for young Paul. The young bastard would surely fritter his chances away. He was too idle and too arrogant to make a good boss. Still, facts were facts. He'd never run stolen cattle on this range again. The whole operation had been blown and the cattle station was no good to him. He must start again somewhere, maybe Montana or Idaho where he wasn't known. He would change his name . . .

Mo Morris, the little man told to watch Maddison saw the wild lunge and the nearly impossible escape of the rancher-rustler. He marvelled at the desperate nerve of the man. It showed although Joss K. Maddison got others to do his dirty work, he could at a pinch move his arse to save his own skin. That was why he'd shuffled through the heap and become top dog. Little Mo went looking for

Buscadero who was busy exchanging target practice with a set of ruffians who should have known better.

He grunted when Mo shouted in his ear what he'd seen.

"Take over here, I'm going after him," said Buscadero, and left Mo squinting down his rifle at a rustler's exposed backside.

Joss K. was limping along wearily still immersed in gloomy thoughts of what he was leaving behind when he heard hoofbeats behind him. He turned in the saddle and saw by the fast strengthening daylight the galloping figure behind him. The man wore black, no glint of tell-tale metal or colour about him. His heart missed a beat and then rage overwhelmed the sudden fear and he wheeled away to a small ravine covered in bush, smothering a small stream already muddied by countless beasts who'd drunk there. It was one of the main watering-holes on this range. He was well acquainted with it, and the narrow defile at the far end where a man could climb out and a fresh horse could follow.

But the horse wasn't fresh. A man could climb out on his own but he would be stymied if he hadn't a horse to ride. The sun would see to that.

That was his first mistake.

The second was that the man following him knew the ravine better than he did. He'd played there as a youngster.

Maddison skirted the soft churned mud of a thousand hooves and pushed his way into the interior. He grinned. He could pick off the cursed Buscadero at his leisure. He knew of a ledge only yards from the entrance. He could hole up there, give the gelding time to rest and feed and before he left he could water him. No problem.

He tied his horse in a patch of grass well into the ravine where the beast wouldn't hear the approaching horse and nicker in greeting. He wanted no giveaway. Then, moving swiftly and past caring about hiding trail he crossed to the other side of the ravine, and up the steep crag to a ledge that had been used many times as a lookout by his own men when on a count of heads.

He inspected his Colts and hastily jacked in shells, also the Winchester which was more important. He wanted the gunhawk with his first shot if possible, while Buscadero was still unaware. He settled down to wait and it was then reaction set in.

He trembled. He couldn't control his limbs. He cursed under his breath. If only he had a shot of something to calm him down! But he had nothing, not even his water bottle, and in the urgency of leaving his horse he'd not drunk from the stream . . .

The silence was nerve-racking. A gecko slid away from him towards the stream, and later a gopher came and raised his head and stared at him, only to dart away when he moved his hand. Up above, the sun rose high and somewhere nearby were the remains of something that had been dead for more than two days. It stank to high heaven and later on a buzzard came down to investigate and another joined him and Maddison could see if he craned his neck how the birds fought over the meat . . .

Maddison was sweating. Surely Buscadero was in the ravine. He calculated that it must be two hours since his arrival, and still no sign of the man who must have seen the angle in which he'd ridden and guessed at the ravine. What the hell was he playing at?

A stranger would have galloped in, forced his way through the brushwood and followed the path of the stream and passed the little hollow below where Maddison would have had time to take deliberate aim and blow the bastard to hell.

His dry tongue passed over equally dry lips. That had been a bad mistake. He hadn't figured on being holed up so long. His body dripped sweat and he knew if he didn't drink soon he would be completely dehydrated. He knew what would happen then. He considered going down to the stream below. It was tantalising to see the steady stream of water and hear the trickle as it ran over the stoney bed. Jeeze! What he would give for a cool glass of water!

The trickle of water down in the ravine seemed to be louder now. The sun had moved over the floor of the natural cleft highlighting the stream. It was beckoning him, tantalising him to a point of mad recklessness. To hell with it! Maybe he was being a fool. Buscadero must have passed on, unable to find his way into the opening or just too ignorant to realise that the stream was only the mouth of a small box canyon.

He decided to scramble down the loose shale at a spot deeper inside the ravine. He should descend to a small pool if his reckoning was correct. He moved slowly and warily and as the silence grew as the birds and all living things grew silent as if listening, he became bolder in his eagerness to plunge into the precious water.

Crouching low, he scrambled and by clinging with one hand to tufts of gama grass he gradually angled down towards the overhung pool. As he came closer he was conscious of an old familiar stench of hot sun on rotting meat . . .

Panic caught at his throat. Dear God in heaven, don't let it be in the pool . . . But when he reached the silent deadly place he knew before he saw it, the pool was defiled. But the horror was all the greater when he saw what polluted the lapping water . . . the horse that he had tethered just hours ago, swollen and already bloodying the water from gaping wounds caused by small predators attracted by the new blood. Flies buzzed about the slit throat and soon, very soon when the wind carried the rich taint up above to bounce off the crag above the buzzards would come down and fight for the carcase.

His thirst was increased by his exertions. He sobbed. The plan was to go on, fight his way through the prickly pears and the greasewood and find the path that led to the narrow trail which led upwards and out of the ravine. But to be successful he had to have a horse to ride those exposed miles back to the ranch. Now . . .

He screamed and cursed Buscadero in as loud a voice as his choking throat would allow. Fury was burning him up and in the middle of a paroxysm of maniacal rage when he'd stopped to draw breath, he heard laughter. It was so shocking in its sinsiter overtones that it froze the blood in his veins. Then a bullet slammed into the rock beside him and then as he instinctively ducked the other way there came another and another, and he knew the man firing the gun was playing with him.

He scrambled a little further amongst the scree, the blood pounding in his ears. Where the hell was the bastard?

Another bullet hummed past his head to explode the rock nearby into a thousand lethal shards. He dropped his rifle and lunged for it as it tumbled dangerously near the edge of the steep slopping animal trail. If he lost that, he lost all hope of getting out of this mess alive.

For the first time it came to him that maybe he wouldn't come out of this no matter how crafty he might be. Maddison wasn't used to being on the losing side. Usually he had the men he paid well for facing this kind of situation. But now it was his carcase on the line. He swallowed, trying to conjure up spit in his mouth. He must communicate with the devil lurking down there amongst the undergrowth.

His mind was every which way to devise any cunning scheme that might have the faintest chance of succeeding. He was catching at ideas like catching gnats in the wind . . .

"Buscadero . . . come out. I want to talk to you." His voice croaked like a bull-frog's. There was no answer. Desperately Maddison tried again. His throat felt as if it was sliced by glass.

"Buscadero, you bastard. I know you're there. What about a deal? I can make you a rich man."

A bullet whined above his head. He cursed and hefted the rifle. If the bastard once showed himself, he'd blast his head off, no matter what the deal . . .

"Come on, man. You don't realise just how rich I can make you. What do you say to a hundred thousand dollars?" Silence. "You bastard! I'll make it two hundred thousand!"

Two slugs came this time and both closer than the last. He had to move and move fast. He took a deep breath and scuttled further along the path, always climbing. His heart was pumping horrifically what with his thirst and the effort of scrambling upwards. He knew his blood was thickening. He was also having dizzy spells when he had to hang on to himself by burying his teeth into his underlip for the pain to keep him conscious.

"What will it take for you to lay off this crazy hunt? What is it with you, man, that you should make it a personal grudge? I'm nothing to you . . . " This time it brought forth a response from down below. He couldn't pinpoint the sound. The towering cliffs echoed and the harsh voice bounced around and above. Bewildered, Maddison could only listen, his rifle ready for the first indication of his torturer s location.

"That's where you're wrong, Maddison. I'm everything to you, feller. I'm the little future you've got left. Think on it, buster. I'm your ultimate fate!"

"What are you talking about? I'm nothing to you. I'd never heard of you until you rode into Greenwater Spring."

Harsh laughter greeted these words.

"You're going to die, Maddison. Tomorrow or the next day. Not today, it would be too soon."

"Why?" screamed Maddison. "Are

you loco? What have I done to you personally? A man doesn't take this kind of revenge just because he kidnaps some two-bit local girl! Betsy Yates is nothing to you . . . "

"She was my pard's daughter. I owed her. Today's little hunt is dedicated to her. Tomorrow is dedicated to another woman . . . "

"What the hell do you mean, another woman? Are you in league with Carrie Smithers? By God, that's it, isn't it? The bitch put you up to this! How much is she paying you to kill me? I can double or treble it. As I said I'm willing to pay two hundred thou . . . "

"Forget it, shitshanks. Money doesn't come into it."

"Then what do you want?"

"You on a spit!"

Panic and desperation exploded in Maddison's brain. He jacked the lever of the Winchester and fired repeatedly into the bushes down below, until the weapon was empty, in a fan-shaped swathe, and then dropped the weapon

151

at his feet and sank down behind a jutting rock, a pitiful defence if Buscadero really wanted to kill him.

But his words came back to give him a tingle of hope. Today Buscadero had stated was not to be the day of his death. He could run and though the shots might come, the fiend wasn't shooting to kill, only to scare the shit out of him. He would take advantage. His eyes glaring with a mad light, and his dry lips stretched back in a mad grin, Maddison crouched and ran leaving his empty rifle behind.

He wanted water. He was going to get it. He would make for up-stream where the water was pure. He laughed and the sound carried and Buscadero detected the hint of madness and all the desperation the man was feeling. He smiled. Maddison would suffer far more than his mother did . . .

Buscadero watched the fugitive and calmly drank from his waterbottle. He must be enduring untold agonies knowing water was so near. He would be able to smell it . . . He drew a careful bead six inches to the left shoulder and at the last minute moved it a fraction. The slug slammed into the good shoulder seconds before Maddison heard the report. He screamed and punched the rock behind him. It jetted him forward to the very edge of the path and he lay and looked down into the narrow strip that was the floor of the ravine. Stunted trees would have broken his fall but they might have acted as spears and punctured his body like a pepperpot. He lay and trembled, his numbed shoulder not yet sending pain signals to his brain.

He struggled to his knees and hung on to a rough ledge and faced the ravine.

"Why don't you show youself, Buscadero? You've got a reputation as a fast gunman. Are you really a yellowbellied bushwacker? Is that how you got your notches on your gun?"

The cool amused laughter struck

terror into Maddison's heart. He'd figured the gunman would have come out guns blazing. At least he might have plugged Buscadero or been killed nice and quick himself. Anything was better than this, and Buscadero had said it would last another three days!

"What's so funny?" he screamed. "Why don't you come out into the open? Goddammit! you can't be frightened of a wounded man!"

"You're right, Maddison. I'm not frightened of you, wounded or not. Before the day's over, I'll shoot you in your feet, and then it will be your kneecaps. I'll leave your right arm free. You can kill yourself at any time . . . "

"You said you would give me today!"

"Yes, but I didn't say I wouldn't take potshots at you. I said I wouldn't *kill* you!"

"You're mad! You know that?"

"You haven't asked me who the other woman was. Tomorrow . . . "

"Yes, who the hell is she if she isn't

Carrie? You and Carrie don't know each other well enough for you to kill me for her unless money was involved."

"Good. Now you're beginning to use your brains."

"Who is she, Buscadero?"

"Do you remember a woman called Louise Juantes?"

For a moment Maddison's mind was blank. Louise Juantes? What the hell was he talking about? Then the name Juantes sounded a warning note in his head and the warning became louder as memory returned. Juantes! That was the name of the man his father had burned out and killed to take over the small farmstead and grab the range that ran alongside it more than twenty years ago . . . Then he remembered something else. The woman. The New England wife of the Mex who'd been so snooty . . . a daughter of a Bible-bashing preacher. She'd been a good looker in a frigid goody-goody kind of way. He'd been a young buck in those days. His father had looked on as he and the other men in the outfit had subjected her to a bit of rich ripe loving. It had lasted a couple or three days before ironhorse Williams finally wore her out. Yes, he remembered Lousie Juantes.

He swallowed hard. The name brought back memories he'd rather not remember.

"Why ask me about Louise Juantes? I never knew her."

"You're a liar. You were there the day your father killed mine and burned down the little cabin on the site where your ranch is now. It was the Juantes farmstead your father took over."

"He had the right! Your father was a squatter . . . a nester. He was claiming a range he couldn't use!"

"Whatever he was, it was his land, and you and the men in your outfit subjected Louise Juantes to a degrading nightmare before she died. Do you deny it?"

"I was young. There were men older

than me. I only went along with the others."

"Your father watched and encouraged you. You and your father could have stopped those men."

"We couldn't have stopped a dozen men when they're in rutting mood! Have a heart, Buscadero! Men will be men. Anyhow, it was a long time ago. Why bring it all up now?"

"Because, scumbag, Louise Juantes was my mother. I was the teenage son who happened to be out on the range mending fences!"

Maddison's heart missed a beat and then started pounding. He'd told his father at the time it was a mistake not to round up the kid and kill him, but the boy had vanished and his father had told him to leave well alone. Now it was all coming back to blow up in his face. He drew his Colt and fired, fanning the bushes in a hopeless attempt to kill his tormentor.

"Go on, kill me!" he screamed, and made a mad scramble in a bid to make for the source of running water he could hear so tantalisingly down below.

Cool calculated laughter was his only answer. He knew he was Buscadero's plaything. He began to sob.

8

JACK CALORHAN reined in his horse for a breather on a high ridge. It had been a long gruelling ride for both man and beast. He could see the long straight railroad track which glinted silver where the morning sun touched it. Hazy smoke from the engine stack hung over all. He screwed up his eyes against the glare. He could see the remains of the herd gathered at one side of the track and the tiny figures on horseback controlling the flow as the beeves were herded forward. They were like scurrying ants.

There was no gunfire. He felt a glow of satisfaction. The battle must be over and his good friend, Danny Wesler, State Marshal, must have been there ready to lend Buscadero and the deputies a hand. It had been a good wheeze to get the ranchers there hidden in the boxcars ready to claim their stock.

He watched and saw that the loading was certainly going ahead. Probably the ranchers had said it was better for the arrangement to stand and take their profits back east rather than try and cut out their own beeves from the mixed herd.

He heeled his horse and now the travelling was easier for the gradient was gradual. Half an hour should see him at the cutting. He wondered about Buscadero and Maddison. Had the bastard been killed in the short sharp skirmish or had Buscadero restrained his natural urge to kill and was he holding the bastard for trial?

Danny Wesler and the men with him greeted Calorhan with a grin. Danny, holding out a big hand, gripped his in a bone-crushing vice. Then slapping his back he boomed,

"Glad to see you, feller. We've got some satisfied ranchers here. Maddison sure saved these guys the trouble of driving their herds to the railroad! They're all grateful for what you did, feller. They want to buy you a drink!"

"Not my doing. You've got to thank Buscadero for setting it up. I only thought of the guys helping you out. Where's Buscadero? I want a word about Maddison and what he intends to do now."

Danny fingered his chin and pulled at his walrus moustache as he did when he was figuring something puzzling.

"I don't rightly know, Jack. When Maddison and his men came storming in and we opened up in the boxcars, all hell broke loose. We weren't only trying to blow each other to bits, we had the herd to contend with and you know what it means to have a herd panic. They were all on top of each other and milling around and it was a case of not getting crushed."

"What you trying to say, Danny?"

"Well, during the blasting and firing, I saw Buscadero heading after Maddison. It seems by what one of Buscadero's

161

men said, that Maddison escaped by hanging on between two horses and being carried out of the crush. Buscadero saw him and followed. Neither of 'em's been seen since."

"Shit!" Calorhan hawked and spat on the ground.

"Maddison must have got clean away and Buscadero's gone after him. Unless of course, Buscadero's copped it?"

Danny shook his head. "We've looked around but Buscadero's not amongst the dead. We gotta heap of bodies over there," nodding at a small stand of stunted trees, "and there's no fear of them swelling up and bursting for a few hours when they're in the shade. You can look 'em over, but the deputies says Buscadero or Maddison's not amongst 'em."

Fair enough. I think maybe I should look around. Buscadero could be laid hurt somewheres. He could have bought one . . .

"Can't go by sign, Jack. There's been too much milling about. Some of the beeves jumped the wire. There's dead cows hung up and others hanging about and the coyotes are closing in. We heard a couple of packs howling during the night . . . "

"Doesn't sound good, if a guy's laid out helpless like. I think I'll just change horses and go for a look-see."

"Just as you wish, Jack. You want for me to send a deputy with you?"

"No. I'll figure it best on my own. I'll just have a quiet sniff around."

He stayed with the jubilant men long enough to devour a plate of biscuits and drink a couple of mugs of strong black coffee which one of the deputies had conjured up for the benefit of the whole outfit.

The meal lifted the weariness in him. It had been a long night. His wits were already blunted from the hours playing poker. His body ached and he could have done with a few hours rest but the men's disappearance niggled him.

He rode out and when he was a half-mile from the cattle enclosure he circled about and made a painstaking search for sign of horses riding away from the cutting. He'd nearly given up hope when he came upon a distinct set of hoofprints of a newly shod horse. His spirits lifted. Perhaps this was a breakthrough. There wouldn't be much traffic for horsemen in the remote part of the range. Whoever had ridden that horse, and someone had, because of the depth of the marks in the soft earth, he followed the tracks and found that the reason for the soft ground was that a small stream petered out disappearing into the more arid ground at this point. He backtracked this ground and soon he saw that it was a drinking area for the cattle on this range. The horse tracks disappeared amongst a lot of other animal tracks but every now and again, a distinct horseshoe imprint could be seen. It was plain that whoever was riding was trying to stay on hard ground. Then suddenly it dawned on Calorhan that he was following two distinct sets of

164

hoofprints. One set was larger than the other, and one had a front left shoe that was worn.

Now he knew he was on the right track.

The soft ground grew into a wider area and led into an overgrown ravine. It could hardly be called a canyon, its walls were not tall enough. The soft ground now gave way to a fast-flowing stream which had encouraged the lush greenery. It was hard pushing a way through the undergrowth but there were signs that someone had gone before him.

Cautiously he moved ahead and a couple of hours passed before he came on the stinking horse.

He gagged. It was obvious the swollen up belly had burst and blood and gore surrounded the area. Wild animals had dragged entrails away from the carcase and even now buzzards flapped overhead, disturbed by his coming. He hastily moved on, but more cautiously than ever. Somebody was out there and they would be desperate. If it was Maddison, then he would have to watch his back as well as his front. If it was Buscadero, then he would still be in danger for Buscadero would fire first and ask questions afterwards.

It was suffocatingly hot. The heat seemed to bounce from the sides of the ravine and flies and insects disturbed by his passing settled on the sweat on his body. He found a small patch of grass and tethered his horse. It would be easier to explore on foot. Taking his waterbottle and hefting his rifle after checking it for loads, he moved forward Indian style.

A horse whinnied to his far left. It seemed to come from a distance, but sounds could be deceiving in this gash in the natural terrain. Then came the sporadic gunshots coming from God knows where for the high rise cliffs distorted the sound and direction.

He swore. That meant both men were alive and one was stalking the other. Who had lost his horse? He was going to have to be doubly careful in his approach.

He found signs of footprints and the place where someone had scooped up water perhaps filled his water bottle. He had no means of knowing who he was following. He had the growing feeling that whoever was out there stalking the other was playing a cat-and-mouse game. Whoever it was, was a cold deliberate killer. He knew Buscadero. The first time they met, they tangled, one on each side of the law. It had taken several meetings, mostly concerned with the handing over of wanted criminals, before their respect for each other had turned to friendship. But Buscadero was no cold killer. He brought his men in alive to stand trial. He was not emotionally involved. They were just so much merchandise to him and as long as he collected his bounty he would ride away satisfied.

Buscadero never went hunting trouble. He was a genial man in drink and a good companion. He and Buscadero had spent many rowdy evenings together and on occasion turned several nasty situations into peaceful solutions. Buscadero had the gift of the gab and could cool hot tempers.

But he had seen Buscadero's other darker side. He'd seen him shoot down a man like a man shooting a rat. Deliberate, coldly and with clinical expertise and the hot slugs slamming past his head had not made him dodge in the doing of it. His very coolness had won the day, for the sadistic monster had been too rattled to take aim.

The deliberate coldness had impressed him more than any fancy shooting. Buscadero had been oblivious to his own risk. He acted like a man who had an invisible shield about him.

But now . . . he didn't think a man like Buscadero would stalk a man like some savage animal. He would come out into the open and give Maddison a chance to give himself up. If the chance was refused then he would go in with guns blazing and finish the job.

Therefore, he figured, it must be Maddison stalking Buscadero for some reason of his own.

He moved slowly on for a few fraught yards and then stopped to sniff the air and listen. His ears ached with the effort. He wasn't cut out for this sweat-making fear-inducing kind of stuff. He was more familiar with the cattle-town shoot-outs. He reckoned it was safer having a brawl on a Saturday night and half a dozen drunken cowpunchers blazing away like a lot of kids, than skulking around in this stinking oven of a place expecting a bullet in the back at any minute. If it wasn't for ride and a certain stubbornness, he would have led Buscadero to his own devices. But Buscadero was his friend and worth a bloodletting for. He spat and took a drink and moved on.

His boots scraped on a rock. The sound was intensified. He froze. A vulture flapped clumsily up into the air as if disturbed and nearby a lizard slipped hastily away into the cooler depths of the rocks below.

Suddenly a slug whipped past his head. He ducked. No time to be a hero. His own rifle came up but there was nothing to see ahead, only the blue haze of rifle fire. His teeth grated. Whoever was doing the hunting wasn't going to make a mouse out of him! He fired at the haze blindly. If the bastard was going to risk another shot he would hold him down . . . then he rolled under a clump of prickly mesquite and cursed as the needles tore his flesh. At this rate the bloody vultures would be sitting patiently waiting to tear out his guts. They could smell blood for miles.

"Maddison, if that's you back there, you'd better come out," he shouted firmly, "It's all over back at the ranch. I'm taking you in."

A black clad figure stepped from behind a rearing slab of rock which a startled Calorhan had thought was one long continuing cliff face. In a flash his Winchester came up and he

170

took aim. His finger tightened on the trigger when a strong voice barked.

"Hold it! What you doing here, Jack? Goddamnit! I could have killed you."

Calorhan's finger relaxed and the gun barrel was lowered.

"Hell! Buscadero, it's you! I had you figured for Maddison!" The reaction was so sharp and the relief gut-grinding he was going to need the crapper. He crawled nearer so that they didn't have to bawl across the ravine at each other.

Buscadero stretched, but did not grin.

"It's a long story, Jack and there's no time to tell it. I've got Maddison bottled up. There's nowhere for him to run but up there," and he nodded towards the fast narrowing gorge where the stream ran narrow and deep and swiftly, and the sides were sheer wet rock, perpetually drenched in spray, and the atmosphere fogged and hazy. A mesh of shrubs grown big because of permanent water made climbing difficult. Buscadero indicated to Calorhan to come and take a look-see.

He climbed a jutting pinnacle and looked upwards. There, beyond rifle range, was the tiny figure of Maddison which had been hidden from his view further down the gorge. He was clinging to the slippery rocks, feet splayed and one arm hanging loosely by his side.

"Looks as if you've hit him again, Buscadero."

"Hmm, enough to make life difficult. I meant to bust his ankles and then his knee-caps but the wily bastard slipped behind the rocks and got away."

"You could take him out now. Why don't you?"

Buscadero's grin made Calorhan shudder. Was this the same man he called friend? He looked again at Maddison and wondered why he was so different from all the other wanted men Buscadero had gone after.

"I've got my reasons," and Buscadero stared at the tiny struggling figure who moved upwards another foot. Then he slipped and slithered downwards a couple of feet and started again. "One up two down," Buscadero muttered. "Just think, Jack, that bastard has had no water for more than thirty hours. He'll be drinking in the fog and thinking it's nectar! What do you think he'll be suffering, eh?"

Calorhan looked at him with horror. "That's not like you, Buscadero. Have you gone mad? Is it because the bastard kidnapped that girl of Yates'?"

The hard dark face did not soften. The eyes were veiled. Calorhan couldn't really tell what the man before him was thinking. He wasn't elated at Maddison's long-drawn-out torture. It didn't please him. He acted like a man who was making sure the punishment was being meted out in full measure.

"Betsy Yates? I suppose she does come into it. Davey made me responsible for her. He was my good friend and I was sorry I didn't breeze in sooner and save her from Maddison's abuse and all that

173

followed. But Betsy's a survivor like her father. She'll not break because of Maddison. No . . . there's another reason, a private reason."

Calorhan contemplated him for a long moment.

"It must be a bloody serious one. But I'll not pry, but I must say I don't like what you're doing or what you've become!"

"Suit yourself! What you think won't make the slightest difference. Maddison will die but only when I'm ready to let him die!"

"Jesus, Joseph and Mary! What the hell have you become, Buscadero?"

9

THEY watched until the sun cast long shadows along the wall of the crag. Twice Buscadero aimed a shot almost casually at the now weary figure making his despairing ascent. It was as if the man's muscles refused to do his bidding, his legs sprawling in ungainly positions. The first shot had made him jump and slip. He'd had enough fight in him to twist about producing his Colt and firing wildly until the slugs were done. Then he'd thrown it defiantly from him and it had tossed and whirled to be lost in the undergrowth below.

"Bastard!" he'd called. "Why don't you have done?" His voice echoed as it bounced between the jagged cliffs.

"Why don't you jump?" and Buscadero's laughter sounded demoniacal as if thunder and lightning would follow.

Calorhan turned away. This was none of his business but this cold-blooded psychological torture was only something he'd read about, mainly in dime novels. He'd never witnessed it before. He was a fist-and-gun man, meting out physical punishment. What he was witnessing was something you wouldn't allow to happen to a wounded horse!

He opened up his warbag which he'd had the foresight to strap to his back. He would settle for a chew at some strips of jerky. They would settle the stomach grumblings. But Buscadero grinned.

"You came prepared. Have you coffee in there?"

"Yeh, I always carry some possibles. Tobacco too. Want some?"

"Doesn't matter about tobacco. I can smoke it or leave it alone. It's coffee I want. Besides, I want the hot rich brew to waft itself up there to the ledge where that goddamn rapist is!"

Colorhan watched him narrowly as

he brought out the old black coffee-pot and then gathered some dry grass and twigs to start a fire.

"So it *is* the girl? She's what this is all about?"

Buscadero did not answer but grabbed up the coffee-pot and made his way down to the stream. When he came back he settled the pot on the flames and for a few moments gazed into the crackling flames. Then he looked at Calorhan with a great weariness, and Calorhan was struck by his haunted eyes.

"You're wrong. When Maddison's father fired his ranch and killed my father, he and this bastard here . . . took my mother . . . She lasted . . . three days. There were over twenty men . . . Can you imagine . . . ?" He turned away, his jaw tight.

Calorhan felt the searing shock go through him. Jeeze! He'd had no idea. No wonder Buscadero was the cold devil he was! If he hadn't been, he would have exploded.

"What about . . . you?"

Buscadero stared stonily into the flames as if he could see everything clearly again.

"I was out on the range. The old man had fenced in some land to run a few cows and the fence was to stop the critturs from raiding the fields. They was constantly breaking through and it was one of my jobs to ride around them and repair any holes. I was half a day's ride away when they came. I started back when I saw the smoke. I knew something was wrong but I couldn't get back to help."

"You couldn't have done much against a whole outfit," Calorhan said gruffly.

"I realised that. I lay low amongst the rocks, high enough to watch the smouldering ranch. Only one barn away from the main buildings was intact. I saw the body of my father laid outside. I wanted to ride down with guns blazing and take his body, but I was only fifteen. I was sick to my stomach. I could hear screaming and them singing and shouting, and then my mother somehow managed to run half naked out of the door into the yard and that bastard up there ran after and dived at her legs . . . He . . . he took her on the ground and then carried her back inside. He was worse than a beast . . . At least beasts know when it is the right time to mate. They don't torture their mates afterwards."

There was a long silence. Calorhan spat out the jerky. Suddenly he wasn't hungry any more. He could see the woman . . . Slowly he raised his eyes to the dark blob he could just make out clinging to the cliff. Then he said quietly,

"What happens when he reaches the top?"

Buscadero gave his wolfish grin.

"We ride after him. He'll have to walk."

"But how? No horse can get up there!"

"This is where old roots matter! I

know every inch of this country. A quarter-mile back there is a zigzag dry stream bed. I explored it as a boy. These Maddisons never took time out to explore what they held. Too busy creating merry hell and rustling someone else's hard-earned stock. It's possible to climb that dry gulch and lead a horse, even a packhorse can scramble up. Would have made a difference if Maddison had known. I might just tell him about what he missed!"

"Yeh, you do that. It will make him mighty happy!"

Buscadero didn't like the ironic tone. "Something bothering you, Jack?"

Calorhan shrugged broad shoulders. "I still don't like this cat-and-mouse game. I'm sorry and shocked about your ma, but if you get a polecat in your sights, you kill it with a clean shot!"

"He's not a polecat. He's the devil's spawn!"

It was a long night. Dawn couldn't

come too soon for Calorhan. He was getting too old for this lark. Revenge did not keep him warm as obviously it did for Buscadero. They brewed more coffee. They needed it. Calorhan wondered what shape Maddison would be in. The smell of the coffee must be sending him crazy.

He saw that Maddison had moved upwards another eight feet and if his strength held out, with a bit of luck the man would be at the top of the ridge in a little more than two hours. But his ordeal would not be over. It would just take on another shape. He would have to walk in the sun without protection. The way would lead down to the plain and it was forty miles from the homestead. Calorhan reckoned he could never make it.

Buscadro drew on a cigarette, calculating his chances.

"I'll give him one last reminder that we're on his tail . . ."

"No!" Calorhan spoke forcefully, his hand reaching for his Colt.

Buscadero saw the action and frowned. "You taking his side?"

"No. The man's got no chance as it is. Let him get on with what he's doing."

"I want him to shit his britches. It'll attract the ants . . ."

"He's probably done that already. Leave him, Buscadero."

They glared at each other, Buscadero's eyes coming to life like two hot coals. But Calorhan stood his ground.

"Don't bring yourself down to his level, man!"

Buscadero swore and turned away in a fury, unable to stand the contempt in his friend's face.

"You didn't see your own mother . . ."

"Goddammit! Buscadero! She wasn't the first woman to be violated!" The man in black's fists balled and his back stiffened. He turned round, his face suffused with colour.

"I should shoot you for saying that! My mother was special!"

"All mothers are special! But the

Maddisons and their crew only did what men do when they're in a bunch and when they're half-crazed with lust and success and the help from the liquor they swigged! Goddmmit, Buscadero, get a hold on yourself! Haven't you ever come across that situation since? How many women have you known, abused and used by men? We've both gone after wanted men whose crimes started from abusing women!"

"Are you making excuses for him? making him one of many?"

"No, Buscadero. He deserves to die. What he did, and the harm he did you as a fifteen-year-old boy knowing what was happening, will never be altered. She's dead after an ordeal I shouldn't like the wickedest woman in the territory to suffer in that way. You can't change that, man. You can't take away a fifteen-year-old's suffering either. But you as a man must make an effort. You're already turning into one of the walking undead! Do you realise that? You've got about as much nerve and feeling as a corpse. You've got to shake yourself loose, Buscadero, or you're lost!"

The hot eyes became cold and blank as he listened to Calorhan's passionate words.

"You think so?" He threw his coffee dregs over the small fire making it spurt and sizzle. "Let's go."

"Buscadero . . . "

The man in black's glance was forbidding. "Not another word! Or I'll blast you and leave you here!"

Calorhan followed in silence. Buscadero's retraced steps was a much easier route than he'd battled through. Soon, both horses were located and then came the long slow trail to the arroyo cutting through the ravine. If Buscadero hadn't known where he was going, he, Calorhan, as a stranger, would never have found the opening. He could well understand the Maddisons and their riders never dreaming there was another outlet.

They climbed upwards in a gradual

winding gradient, the trail obliterated by nonusage. The going was rough. Loose stones caused the horses to slither and they became nervous and high stepping. They disturbed wildlife that wasn't used to man. A rattler sent Calorhan's horse a-trembling and foamed sweat drenched the beast. There was the smell of decay in the air from past years. It was a desolate spirit-chilling place.

Calorhan glanced sideways at Buscadero when they neared the top of the cut, the way broader and easier now.

"This is sure some place for a youngster to explore. What would have happened if you'd busted a leg or killed your horse?" Buscadero shrugged.

"I never thought of the hazards. I don't suppose I should have been found. My old man wasn't a range man. He concentrated on growing dirt crops. He might have hunted me for days and not found me." He gave a bark of cynical laughter. "I was king of this range, a gawky brash kid who never dreamed life could change. It just goes to show . . . " His voice tailed away as he sat his horse broodingly.

At the top of the long slope they stopped to rest the horses. Buscadero made a smoke and then crooked his head to light it in his cupped hands. Then drawing deeply he threw his head back and sighed.

"You know, I always dreamed of building up our small herd. The old man had a few good cows. He was shrewd, even though his heart wasn't in stock-breeding. I like to think he did it for me. Thought maybe some day I should need this range. I wasn't interested in ploughing dirt. Oh, I did what a boy has to do to help his father. I would have got a tanning if I hadn't . . . but it was a new calf that excited me. I had these dreams, you know, of being a cattle baron . . . Funny, isn't it? The old place turned into a rustlers' lair!"

"Not so funny. It wouldn't have

happened if you'd been older. You would have fought back . . . "

"And died! I would have had no chance. I swore I'd come back some day. But as the years passed and the bounty business took off, the knife edge was not so keen." He turned to Calorhan, his face twisted in a wry grimace. "The fast gunman I am today was conceived by the hunger to return and kill those bastards! Then being the best hunter of men blurred the issue. I would have come back at some time, but maybe not yet if Davey and fate hadn't dealt me a hand! Lady Luck plays some funny tricks on a feller!"

"Yeh, you might say that, and Maddison would agree with you!"

Buscadero frowned. "I'm not changing my mind, Jack. Maddison's had twenty years. He didn't give my folks a choice!"

He dug his rowels viciously into his horse's side. He quivered and leaped forward and Calorhan followed more slowly. For a long while they travelled apart, Calorhan about twenty horse-lengths behind, each engulfed in his own thoughts.

This country was haunting Buscadero, smothering him in a black depression that only eased itself by a brutality he'd never realised was within himself.

Calorhan was thinking of a different Buscadero. A good pard, who, after their first confrontation, became a good friend. He was a relentless hunter, but he'd never bushwacked his victim. He'd given him the benefit of a draw. He wasn't like some bounty-hunters who prefered to take their prisoners back as stiffs. He gave them the choice.

He'd also saved Calorhan's life when they'd both been after the same man. A vicious killer, he'd caught Calorhan literally with his pants down. Roger, the ribsticker, had crept up to the crapper out in the yard of the Silver Dollar way back in Wichita and blasted it with a shotgun. That was the time when he'd taken three shots in the torso, but before Roger could slam open the door and finish him off, Buscadero had waded in and pulped the bastard's head like a melon.

Calorhan brooded. No, Buscadero was his pard. They had a good working-relationship. He couldn't let this temporary madness of his break up something that went back years. He spurred his horse forward.

"What about resting up and brewing us some coffee?"

Buscadero eyed him keenly.

"Still figuring out how to stop me?"

"No, just need food and drink. It's a long ride back to Maddison's ranch."

"And you'd have no stomach for food after what's going to happen?"

Calorhan shrugged. "I got me a good stomach, Buscadero. It's not the actions but the thought that sickens me, feller, make no mistake about that!"

He didn't wait for Buscadero's say-so, he angled towards the shelter of some rocks and dismounted. He undid his saddle and rubbed the horse down

189

to prevent saddle sores, then let him loose. He watched while the horse did a little jig and shook himself and then he rolled in the dirt. When he was on his feet again, he came and nuzzled Calorhan.

"You great baby! You know it's oat-feeding time. All right, feller, you'll get your oats," and he brought out the feedbag and poured into it a couple of handfuls of oats from the warbag on the horse's back.

Buscadero grinned, his black mood lifting.

"You sure do spoil that animal of yours!"

"Yeh. We been together a long time. Best horse in the State. A horse you can trust can mean the difference between life and death."

"True, and you can say that of a good pard!" Calorhan glanced sharply at Buscadero who was now unsaddling his own mount.

"Meaning what?" he asked tersely. Buscadero made a gesture.

"Just what I said. We're good pards . . . "

"And that means keeping out of your business?"

"I'd prefer it, Jack. You let me go to hell in my own way!"

"Why hell?"

"Because I've got this demon in me . . . "

"You could settle down and take over this range again. You've got the right . . . "

"No! For me this place is rot and decay! If young Maddison wants it, he's welcome to it. It's cursed . . . "

"Look, you're a young feller. It's time you settled down. There's that Betsy, she sure seemed to like you. Give up the bounty-hunting. Start again. Make something better of yourself. Revenge rots your insides away . . . "

Buscadero moved around, listening to Calorhan's words as he collected brushwood and dead grass to make a small fire. He squatted before it as he struck a match and blew as the grass smoked and burst into flames. Calorhan emptied water from his canteen into the coffee-pot and set it firmly to boil.

"Are you listening to me, feller?"

Buscadero smiled. "Yeh, you're talking like a father, and it's all rot! Can you see me settling down? I've got this dream, about going up into Montana . . . "

"Well then, why don't you do it?"

"Because I'm not old enough, nor have I got a big enough stake saved for the kind of ranch I want! I'll have to be ancient and suffering with piles before I take to a rocking-chair. Then again, I've got this thing eating my guts . . . "

Calorhan was silent as he brought out flour and salt and baking powder and made pone. It would ease the windy rumbles in the stomach. It would fill if not fatten.

Then when the first flapjacks were made, he said tersely,

"You allowed me to stop without argument. I suppose you're calculating how far Maddison will struggle to walk in the sun?"

"Something like that. Did you think I'd forgotten about him? That's a laugh."

"No, I never thought for one moment you'd forgotten him, but maybe you thought I'd not realised the significance of your stopping."

"You wanted to stop, feller. You wanted to eat."

"True. All I'm saying, Buscadero, is kill the bastard and put him out of his misery. He deserves to die. I'm not disputing that. But I don't like this long-drawn out inch-by-inch business. It's not worthy of you, pard. You'd shoot that horse of yours before you'd let him suffer!"

"Yeh, but my horse is my friend and pard, and I don't hurt my friends!"

"Jesus, Buscadero! You're a hard-nosed bastard!"

"I'm sorry you think that. I'm still your friend, remember that."

Calorhan slopped water into his hat and gave the horse a limited drink. He patted the horse's flanks and

193

ran practised hands down withers and fetlocks, feeling for strains. The going had been rough, but the horse appeared sound. Buscadero's feeling for his horse was as nothing to what he, Calorhan, felt for the chestnut gelding. He watched while Buscadero did likewise. Whether the man in black was aware of it or not, his hands were gentle and tender for a man who appeared emotionless and without nerves. Buscadero might be suffering from some kind of frozen trauma but there was a side to him still vulnerable. He could be hurt.

Calorhan's heart lifted. Maybe Buscadero was acting out his fantasies now. When the confrontation with Maddison came, he would do what he would do himself . . .

He hoped so, for he knew what had to be done even if it meant killing his friend.

They rode on, Buscadero half a length ahead. Now he was scouting the skyline for the staggering figure of a lone walker. He hoped he was still alive and hurting. His teeth drew back in a ghastly grin. Oh, he'd be hurting all right! Tough men didn't die after three days of sun. A man was apt to hang on grimly to life, specially if he thought he had a chance. Maddison must be feeling hopeful because he'd not been followed up that ravine and over the rim into the wild down-sloping country that would eventually lead to home.

He would be celebrating his escape.

He would be whipping himself up to stagger and crawl those miles to the ranch and pray that his young brother might organise a search for him . . .

Suddenly he reined his horse and stared. Calorhan pulled up beside him.

"What is it?" The heat haze made everything shimmer. It was like being hammered by an invisible pile-driver that pounded at head and body, dehydrating it until the skin was dry and blistered. He wondered in what condition was the distant dark blob spread-eagled on the ochre-coloured ground.

"He's travelled farther than I expected," was Buscadro's grim answer.

"What are you going to do now?"

"Go see what kind of shape he's in."

Calorhan did not answer but followed the black-clad figure who sat so stiffly aboard his horse.

The distance was deceptive. It was nearly an hour before they'd negotiated the rough terrain and came to stop beside the sun-blackened figure coated with dust and bloodied with his wounds, and that of hands torn in the fight to climb out of the gorge.

He was still alive. He stared at them convulsively, his throat working.

"Water . . . " he whispered in a croak. "Give me water."

Calorhan made to get down from his horse with the intention of giving him a drink.

Buscadero's gun hand came up,

the Colt firmly held in Calorhan's direction.

"Don't waste your water on this scum! It won't help him where he's going now!"

"Aw, to hell, Buscadero, a drink's neither here or there! I can't stand by . . ."

"Going soft? Well, get moving. As we agreed, it's no business of yours!" Then he stepped down from his horse and entwined his fingers in Maddison's shirt and hauled him to his feet. "Walk, you bastard! I want to see you walk!"

Maddison looked groggily at him, his eyes swivelling upwards into his head.

"I . . . I . . ."

"Yes, you can! You can walk. Now move!"

Maddison staggered a few steps forward, weaving like a man drunk, his knees giving under him. Buscadero rammed the gunbarrel into his shoulder-blades and he stiffened and groaned.

"You bastard . . . Buscadero!" but

the momentary flash of fury was short-lived. He fell and Buscadero hauled him to his feet again by his wounded shoulder. It started to bleed again and the blood was a thick sticky mess.

"I might be a bastard, Maddison, but not of your calibre. Remember Betsy Yates, and what she suffered by you and your men? Remember the Juantes woman all of twenty years ago and how you and your father and those scumbags you ran with treated her?"

The ravaged bristled face looked at him with sick puzzlement.

"The Juantes woman? The Mex's wife . . . the white whore . . . "

Buscadero's fist smashed into his jaw, mashing swollen lips. Maddison went down without a sound.

For long moments Buscadero breathed heavily, the hot air searing his lungs, but it was nothing to the white-hot heat of his fury to hear his mother called a whore. Then he dragged Maddison to his feet and his fist again connected to the helpless man's face. This time he spat out several teeth. Buscadero shook him.

"Don't you remember? It was my mother, you goddammed sonofabitch!"

Maddison couldn't stand. He was being held up by Buscadero. His body sagged in on itself.

"You were the kid we couldn't find . . . " His laughter was something to make Calorhan shudder. "I always said it was a mistake letting you live. Pa wouldn't let me hunt you up. He said you were just a kid and no danger . . . " He coughed, as blood ran down his chin from his torn gums. "How wrong he was!"

He looked from Buscadero to Calorhan standing silently watching and waiting.

"You were going to give me water." His smile was ghastly. "As a dying man I should have my last wish. Or are you frightened of this madman here? Maybe you're frightened of his guns?"

"I'm not frightened," Calorhan answered evenly. "It's not my quarrel."

"Then why are you here?"

"I ask myself that. Maybe to see some kind of fair play." Maddison's bleary eyes narrowed, then he turned to Buscadero.

"What are you going to do with me?"

"I'm going to make you walk or crawl back to that ranchhouse you and your father built on the site of my father's shack, and then I'm going to shoot you in front of that good-for-nothing young brother of yours."

"And what about him?"

"Does it worry you about his fate?"

"As a matter of fact it does. He's an ungrateful young swine and a fool but he's all I've got. Besides, he wasn't born until after the raid and Pa took him a new wife. He shouldn't pay." He turned to Calorhan. "You'll see the boy's safe?"

Calorhan nodded. There was no need for words. He was keyed up. There was something else on his mind.

"Buscadero!"

"Yes?"

"Finish it now. Enough's enough!"

"No way! I'm walking him back . . . "

Calorhan's guns came up.

"Then I'll do it myself!" and Maddison smiled and closed his eyes.

Buscadero allowed him to drop to the ground and leapt into a crouch while Calorhan's weapon followed Maddison's inert body. His first shot took Maddison in the heart. The body juddered convulsively. He whipped round and covered Buscadero. Both guns exploded at the same time and incredibly Buscadero's slug missed Calorhan's head by six inches. Calorhan's own shot took Buscadero in the soft part of his shoulder. He cursed as the slug's velocity twisted him around like a ballet dancer before he collapsed to the ground.

"You should thank your gods you were my friend," he gasped. "I could have killed you!"

"Yeh. I didn't think that shot was the best you could come up with! So you do have emotions after all!"

Calorhan leathered his gun and then bent down to see to the damage his slug had inflicted. His fingers probed.

"Goddammit! Mind what you're doing," Buscadero grumbled. "I've got feelings, you know."

"Glad to hear it. I was beginning to wonder. Anyhow, it's only a flesh wound. You'll live. Now it's a case of getting you and this feller here back to that there ranch."

"I'll leave you to worry about the details," and Buscadero promptly fainted.

10

THE swinging bumping sensation ceased and Buscadero opened one eye and found his mouth full of horse's mane. He spat and struggled to sit upright. He was aboard his gelding, bound to him to hold him on, and the ache in his legs and back told him he'd been straddled the bony back for a long long time.

He groaned.

"Did you *have* to string me up like a side of beef?" He was surprised his voice sounded so weak. His shoulder throbbed. Damn Jack Colorhan!

By the dizzy spells he must have lost a bucket of blood. The stupid fool hadn't stopped the copious flow. He could feel it sticky and flyblown down one side of him and along his arm. Some friend!

The mildly humorous voice of Jack

Calorhan came to him in a daze.

"Sure, feller. How else would I get you and this here corpse back to the ranch if I didn't tie you on? I don't aim to be God and work miracles!"

"What we stopping for? I could use a drink."

"You'll get it. We're just coming into the ranch yard. Just watching to see that no stray Maddison dogs have escaped to take potshots at us. There's the little matter of the kid . . . "

Buscadero closed his eyes.

"Don't worry about him. He'll fall apart when he hears about you killing his brother." There was a touch of malice in the words. Calorhan grimaced. Then Buscadero's eyes opened wide. "Just what did you do with him?"

"I told you, or aren't your brains figuring? Brought him back to the ranch. Boy will want to bury him beside his old man."

"I know that, buster, but *how* did you bring him back?"

"Ruined a good rope on the pair

of you. Tied his ankles together and dragged him home. How else?"

Buscadero grunted.

"He don't deserve it. You should have left him for the buzzards!"

"Same old Buscadero! It's a good job I know you."

"Yeh, you can say that. If I hadn't known you, you would have been buzzard meat yourself!"

Calorhan nodded tersely. "I suppose you think I owe you?"

"You might say . . . Aw, to hell, quit talking and let's get to the ranch and give that boy something to chew over. My mind's on water."

Calorhan heeled the chestnut and both horses plodded on. Buscadero wasn't the only one wanting water. Calorhan's dry tongue rasped over dry lips. His waterbottle had been emptied twenty miles back, divided between the two horses. If they'd dropped, they would both have been in trouble.

In front of the ranch-house he halted, the grisly parcel casting up dust. The horses acted nervous. No horse likes an unexplained object bumping and scraping behind them and this one smelled peculiar to delicate horse nostrils. Calorhan got down stiffly, his piles playing up from the close sweaty ride. They itched and he could have done with a scratch. It would be good to lie in a hot tub and soak.

He quietened his own horse and then moved round to the other, his hand smoothing over the sweating rump. It couldn't be easy for a man tied aboard a nervous horse. Not with daylight showing through his shoulder where a slug had torn its way through.

He untied the rope, and supported Buscadero and was for easing him down when a high quavering voice told him to hold it. He turned and saw Paul Maddison holding a shotgun in their general direction. The boy was white-faced and he looked as if he could pull the trigger at any moment.

"Now son, don't be hasty. We brought your brother home."

"He's been found then? There's been a marshal here and his deputies looking for him. They've turned the place over and gone off again, but who . . . " He stopped suddenly. He'd spied the bundle down below behind the horses. "Oh, my God!" and the shotgun wavered dangerously. It went off pointing upwards as Calorhan threw himself up the steps on to the verandah and brought the boy down with a leg tackle.

"Don't be impetuous, boy, or you might not live long," he advised grimly.

"You bastards! You killed him! My brother. I'll get you for this . . . " The boy snarled as he fought the strong hands holding him down.

"Easy talk, boy. You were lucky they were deputies that came here. If it had been the ranchers, they might have strung you up! Now use your brains, kid, and pipe down. Your brother had it coming to him. I brought him back. I could have left him on the range for the buzzards! He's all yours, kid. You can do with him what you like. Who's here with you?"

The boy sobbed.

"Just Cookie. They've all ridden out."

"How many?"

"Our usual six and then another dozen hired."

"You know why?"

The boy's eyed flickered uneasily.

"Look, mister, I don't know anything about my brother's dealing. He kept me out of things. Said I would talk and the less I knew the better. I had nothing to do with anything. I swear it, mister!"

Calorhan looked at him scornfully and then allowed him to rise after taking charge of the shotgun.

"You just enjoyed the situation, didn't you? The brother of a powerful so-called rancher who could call the shots. I understand you were an arrogant little shit. Made trouble down in Greenwater Spring and expected your brother to bale you out! Now you've got *real* trouble and you'll have to sort it out yourself."

"What you going to do with me?" The voice quivered.

"Shit yourself, have you? You smell like it. Son, I don't shoot kids and I don't take in the innocent. As far as I'm concerned you're off the hook. What the townsfolk of Greenwater Spring think, is their business. I'd advise you to lie low for a while."

"But . . . "

"No more kid. I've got a wounded man to see to."

"But I don't know what to do!"

"Then go and see your brother's man of business. He'll advise you. Maybe you should clear out of this neck of the woods for good."

"Oh, God!" and the boy collapsed sobbing on to the wooden boards of the verandah.

Calorhan toed him out of the way while he eased Buscadero out of the saddle and carried him up the steps and into the Maddison living-room and laid him down on a couch that was covered by an Indian blanket.

"Ow, you sonofabitch!" Buscadero groaned. "You've got hands like hayforks!"

"Stop your moaning, feller, and let's have the dirty shirt off before you get blood poisoning."

"What about water?"

"Ah, yes, I'll get the old swamper on the job. He can water the horses too," and he strode outside to the cookhouse and rustled out the half-drunk old cowboy who was drowning out the ugly facts of life. His rheumy eyes flickered.

"What do you want? I know nothing. I'm only acting cook around here. What the boss does, is, or was his business. I see you've got a stiff out there. It's him, isn't it? I know nothing," and he belched and the fumes of rotgut whisky threatened to explode into flame.

"Look, old timer, all we want is a jug of water to drink and a basinful of hot to clean my pard's wound, and maybe some coffee and if you could hustle up some food?"

"Yeh, I can do that an' all. We got some prime steaks ready to grill, newly killed from one of the best beef cattle spreads . . . Eh, I shouldn't be saying that. You'll forget about it, if I cook 'em for you, and I make tolerable biscuits. Food's rough, but I ain't no real cook, Cookie got shot . . . " A glazed eye looked Calorhan over, "I guess you know who did that, so I'll just get on cooking them steaks."

"Good feller. I don't care who's rustled beef it is. Get it on to plates and I'll be blind where you're concerned. Damn me if I won't!"

The hunched up Cook grinned showing gaps in his yellowed teeth. His unwashed body smelled of strong tobacco mixed with the whisky pickle. Calorhan wrinkled his nose, but what the hell . . . he wasn't that particular, his guts reminded him. It had been a long time since his last solid meal.

"Right away, Sir! Water coming up

and might I suggest a snort from this here whisky bottle? Will do your partner a power of good."

"Yeh, now you mention it, it will do us both good!"

The patched-up wound didn't spoil Buscadero's appetite. He sopped up his gravy with the fresh but hard biscuits and gulped down a third mug of coffee and then sighed and lay back replete.

"Jeeze . . . he's a miserable looking little bastard and he stinks like an Indian on a Saturday night but the feller sure can cook steak!"

Opposite him, Calorhan grinned.

"When you start appreciating bad cooking it's time to call it a day and settle down." He glanced at the boy who was sitting moodily beside the wide open wood fire. He was stirring a half charred log and dropping another on top from the log basket. "You, Paul, have you made up your mind what you're going to do?"

The youngster seemed to have aged during the last few hours. Maybe it was the look in the eyes. They were stormy but full of genuine grief.

"Joss brought me up from being a little kid. My pa and ma died when I was five. I'm not leaving this place. I'm going to start from scratch . . . "

"It will be a struggle, boy. This here feller has a legal right to the fields that were farmed and the site of this ranch-house. He was the Juantes boy. You've heard of that family?"

The boy nodded, his eyes wide as he looked at Buscadero. He swallowed hard.

"Yeh, I heard about them, but it was all before my time . . . "

"He might want to settle down, and so turf you out. You can go quiet or . . . " he smiled, "Buscadero has a reputation . . . " Paul Maddison blinked hard. He seemed to cower into little room. Buscadero spat on the floor.

"Aw, quit fooling, Jack. You talk about me being a sadist. What about you? You're frightening hell out of this kid. He's about to wet himself!"

"Look, Buscadero, it's time you settled down. Where better than here, your rightful place? If this kid has any brains, he'll make his way regardless."

"You heard the kid. He wants to start from scratch. Well, I say, all good luck to him. I don't hold grudges against babies born after my folks got killed. I might be a mean bastard, but I'm not a lowdown skunk punishing a kid for what his father and brother did. Forget it, Jack, besides, I'm not ready to settle down!"

"Aw, shit! You're the orneriest sonofagun I've ever come across! What about Betsy Yates?"

"What about her?"

Jack Calorhan rolled his eyes heavenwards, then sighed.

"Hell! If you don't know what I'm talking about, you're not the man I figured!"

Buscadero heaved himself restlessly, angry at himself for his physical weakness.

214

"It's time we were moving and finding out what happened in Greenwater Spring. Danny Wesler will have the whole affair boxed and filed. Are you going to let him take all the glory?"

Calorhan shrugged. "As long as the job's done successfully, what's the odds?"

"You're a darn queer bastard for a lawman!"

"Look who's talking! Well, if you're fit, we'll be on our way." Then he looked at the long face of Paul Maddison. "Cheer up, son. You're young enough to learn that it doesn't pay to be an arrogant pea-brain, and that you've just been dealt the best deal that Lady Luck will ever cast your way. This here feller is willing to forgive and forget where you're concerned. You're keeping your ranch on his say-so and no hassle! Remember that and remember the name Buscadero!" The boy's lips puckered. His eyes flashed in a momentary rebellion and then he controlled his emotion. It was his first act in the transition from boy to man.

"I'll remember and I'll also remember the man who shot my brother!"

"That was an act of kindness, boy. Incredible but true. Think on it."

"I will. Some day . . . "

"Don't say it, son. Words is apt to come back like a boomerang. Just get on with your life."

Buscadero heaved himself heavily aboard his horse. His shoulder throbbed and he was weak from loss of blood but he knew it was clean through which should heal fast. Paul Maddison watched both men ride away. Then old cowboy came and put an arm about the boy.

"Come on, Mr Maddison, there's lots of tidying up to do and decisions to be made."

Paul stared at him, momentarily shocked.

"You called me Mr Maddison!"

"Yeh, why not? You're the boss now. What do you want for your dinner?"

A smile touched the boy's lips and he straightened his shoulders and drew in a long deep breath.

"How about that? Yes, well . . . Can you cook steak and kidney pudding?"

The new Cook smiled.

"I'll have a crack, and while I'm doing the fixin's, maybe you'll do the necessary for your brother." Paul's expression clouded but there was unaccustomed determination there.

"I'll do that, and then we'll make plans. I'll want a couple of new hands. We'll start small and work up. Yes, that's what I'll do. You and me, Cookie, are going to build up a new kind of ranch, the PM Diamond brand. What do you think of that?"

"Yeh, I told your brother years ago he should think up a brand but he just laughed and said why should he? Yours is a good idea, son."

11

"**S**HIT!"

Jack Calorhan faced Betsy Yates in the small hotel bedroom where they'd taken Buscadero protesting and swearing only to collapse weakly on the bed. The ride into town had taken more out of him than he cared to admit.

He lay quietly watching first Betsy and then Jack who was not the calm and shock-proof feller he cracked himself up to be. He was jumping mad and nearly frothing at the mouth. It tickled Buscadero seeing him thus. Serve the big-headed old bugger right! He'd had plenty to say about him and Betsy.

He glanced at her. She was looking prettier than he remembered, or was it his weakness and dependency on her influencing him? His attention was drawn again to Jack as the lawman

218

drew breath and repeated his vitriolic attack.

"The bitch! I'll follow her to hell! There must have been fifty thousand dollars at least in that pot, maybe more! I know I put in ten thousand plus a bank draft and Maddison put in two drafts! Jesus! I didn't reckon that pig-faced porky bitch would run off with a hatful of money! Of all the nerve . . . where was she heading, Miss?"

Betsy Yates lifted her shoulders. She knew but she wasn't telling. A hundred dollars did things to a girl's memory. Besides, she'd liked Carrie Smithers. She was one of the few whores who'd 'bout-faced when she knew the circumstances of the kidnapping and her treatment. Carrie wasn't afraid of opening her mouth. She talked straight. If she hate anyone she did so with gusto, but if she was wrong, she was big enough in every way to admit it.

"I'm sorry I had you figured wrong," she'd said to a bruised and battered

Betsy. "I blamed you for taking him away from me. Maybe you saved me from a beating up. I'm sorry, kid," and those words had forged a liking between them. Now she remained silent. It was one in the eye for all fellers and a boost for women, for Carrie to light out with the gambling lawman's cash. Good luck to her!

"I'll find her! I'll have every sheriff and marshal in Texas looking for her and beyond! I'll have her indicted! I'll see she gets hard labour! I'll . . . "

Buscadero closed is eyes wearily then interrupted his flow.

"Stow it, Jack. You're getting tedious. It's only money. You're always saying that. What the hell . . . think of it as a way of helping another human being. Carrie will make the most of her chances. You'll be responsible for another superior cathouse somewhere!"

He laughed until he hurt as he watched the expression crossed over Calorhan's face. He looked like a constipated drummer who'd lost his medicine samples.

"It's all right for you to make jokes. It's not your money!"

"Some of it wasn't yours either! Remember? Sleight of hand?"

"Aw, to hell with you! I'm going to the telegraph office and send off a few messages. Then I'm looking up the town sheriff and my pal Danny Wesler and rustle up some reward money from those ranchers. Somebody's going to have to pay for this!"

Calorhan went away seething. Then as he walked down the street towards the sheriffs office he was suddenly struck by the ludicrousness of it. Buscadero was right. He was acting like some badly-done-to kid. He grinned wryly, his sense of humour restored. It wasn't many women who put one over on Jack Calorhan!

Then he stopped and lit a cigarette and drew deeply on it and blew blue smoke into the air. What had sent him off half-cock? Then a tantalising vision of Carrie Smithers washed over him, and he choked on his smoke. By Cripes! It was a sense of disappointment that Carrie Smithers wasn't in town and it wasn't because she had a great pair of tits but because he'd thought that for all her brash honesty and big mouth she was some great woman. He was hurt and angry that she was just like all the rest . . .

Angrily he threw down the cigarette stub and ground it into the dust. By hell, he would give her one mighty shock! He'd go after the bitch come hell or high water and he'd paddle her arse, however big she was, and then . . . he grinned and rubbed his tongue round his lips. Maybe it was time he jacked in his badge and found himself a verandah and a rocking-chair and maybe make an honest woman of that aggravating female. She'd put plenty of mileage into her life judging by her age. Maybe she would grab the chance of going legitimate. He rather fancied the fascinating mixture of capable wife cosseting him during the day and athletic whore keeping him happy at night . . .

The first thing was finding the bitch.

He headed for the sheriffs office. Get his finances sorted out and then send off a few telegrams.

★ ★ ★

Buscadero was recovering by the minute. He was actually enjoying Betsy Yates' bullying. He allowed her to feed him and she spent much time in the hotel kitchen concocting nourishing broth to the fury of the resident cook who got in her way deliberately until she threatened to hit him over the head with a ladle.

She was assiduous in her care and attention of Buscadero's wounds, changing bandages twice a day, and he enjoyed her gentle fingers stroking and probing. She made him feel good.

But she became irritating when she opposed his getting up and doing things for himself. He was becoming afraid she was going to insist on giving him a blanket bath and shaving him. Hell! Women were all right in their rightful place which was either caring for a man's stomach or his other more primitive needs, but in between they got so goldarn possessive!

It was high time he high-tailed it. Soft living was a trap. It got to a man all sneaky like. Another reason for taking off into the sunrise was the fact that Betsy Yates was becoming a temptation. He put it down to an overabundance of sap because his body was used to hard work and long hours. If he wasn't careful, he'd be reaching out for her one of these times when she hung over the bed with everything she had hanging temptingly close. He was having a terrible time trying to relax.

"What's the matter, Buscadero? Is the pain bad? You're frowning enough to frighten Geronimo himself. I'm sure the wound is healing well." The gentle hands peeled back bandages and prepared to smear ointment.

"I'm fine, Betsy. I was just thinking."

"Not bad thoughts surely?"

"Nope! Just that I've been lying here too long. I'm going to be up and . . . "

"Oh! But you can't. I won't allow it. It'll take another day or two. You've been through a lot . . . "

"Betsy, my girl, you're talking through your hat! I've had worse wounds than these and I've never even laid low."

"But you'll recover quicker. You'll get your full strength back sooner. I know!"

"Betsy, honey, I've already got my strength back." Her eyes opened wide, but she didn't read any double meaning in the words. Buscadero sighed. It was a time like this when he wished his friend Davey's daughter had been another Carrie Smithers. Well, she wasn't, even though there had been that one episode which for some reason always made him feel ashamed to think of. She'd certainly wanted it, but maybe it had been a reaction to what she'd been through. At least he'd made it enjoyable for her and blotted out the rapes and the disgust and terror of that bad time. He'd done that for her.

The trouble was he couldn't blot out his own experience. The touch and feel of her body was with him every time she came near. But taking advantage of her again would give her ideas. Betsy was a girl who would expect marriage and that word made him shy away like a troubled colt.

The danger signals had gone up.

It was time he was gone.

There was another man to hunt somewhere and someone to pay him for the hunting.

"Buscadero, I've never known your real name. What is it?"

He moved uneasily and then stiffened as she wound bandages about him.

"What's it matter? I haven't heard my name in years."

"I should like to call you by your real name."

"Listen, Betsy, I'm not going to be

226

around long enough for you to call me anything."

She pouted and looked mutinous. "I'd still like to know your name."

He sighed. It would be churlish to refuse her.

"My mother called me Edward. My father called me Eduardo. Take you pick."

"Which do you like?"

Buscadero sighed again. This was ridiculous. "Edward, I suppose. My mother was from New England. I liked the clipped way she said it. Father was Mexican and he gave it a slow musical sound which as a boy I thought wasn't macho. Foolish really."

"I'll call you Edward, or Ed if you prefer it?"

"Look, Betsy, I gave you your father's roll and now it's up to you to get on with your life. I'm not responsible for you. You can go where you please."

"Would my father want that? Didn't he tell you to look after me?" She sounded hurt and somehow vulnerable. Oh, hell!

"Well, yes, I suppose he did in a way, but he wouldn't mean I'd have to take you with me like some kind of adoptive daughter. He knew what kind of life I lead. He just meant I should see you safely on your way."

"To where?"

Buscadero shrugged and the movement hurt his shoulder. "How the hell do I know?" Now he was getting irritable. The fool girl was making him feel guilty as if he was letting both her and Davey down! He knew damn well that Davey hadn't meant him to take her on. Blast it, she would be so much dead weight to carry around, like that old man of the sea he'd heard about who carried a weight on his shoulders.

"You wouldn't leave town and not let me know . . . Edward?"

It sounded funny hearing his name on a woman's lips. It had been so long.

"Now what on earth made you think I might?" He felt guilty as hell for that was what he'd been proposing to himself.

She shrugged.

"Carrie Smithers blew. It seems the easiest thing to do if you want to dodge someone, and maybe you want to dodge me? Do you, Edward?"

"Cree-ist! You do think up some fool things!"

"That's no answer. When I think of . . . that night . . . you know . . . I've been wondering . . . "

"Now look, Betsy, forget what happened. We was both emotional and I'll not take advantage of a young girl . . . "

"That's just it! I'm frightened you think you took advantage. You didn't! I wanted it to happen regardless of what went before! I think I love you, Edward. If you were to ask me to marry you, I should. Now, do you think me very forward? When it comes to hitching up I know men are supposed to be the ones to make the decision. I'm only telling you what I would say if you did ask." There was appeal in her voice. Buscadero felt he'd turned into a stinking swine.

"Now, Betsy, don't take on. Some day you're going to hate yourself for what you're saying now. There's lots of men wanting to settle down with a pretty girl like you."

"But you don't want to settle down?" The words faltered. He knew she was close to tears.

"You're only a kid. I'm nearly as old as your father. Hell, girl, you don't want to take the first man who happens to be nice to you!"

"It's not because we . . . er . . . made love. That makes it better of course but it wasn't that I think you're obligated to marry me. It's just . . . I don't know how to put it into words. I just love you, I guess."

"Betsy, you've got an awful lot of living and loving to do yet. Wouldn't it be better if you hauled in your reins a bit and took it easy? Now if you don't mind, you'd better go now. I'm going to get up and buy myself a drink."

"Why didn't you say? I'll go and buy your liquor . . . "

Buscadero sighed. "Betsy, just get to hell out of it!"

She looked hurt. "I was only trying to be useful."

"And indispensable. I know."

She flushed and bit her lip. She wasn't being very subtle. She wished she were more like the experienced Carrie Smithers.

She smiled through her chagrin. She knew something he didn't know.

No matter what he said, she was going to follow him. She would wear him down. She would learn how to handle him. She would make him feel the boss in their relationship. In reality she would let him out and reel him in, just like a fish on a hook. Buscadero would soon be just another man on a long list of long-gone heroes.

Somewhere, Edward Juantes was

going to put down roots and he would need a wife to do so. She intended to be that wife . . .

He was weaker than he expected. Damned woman! Treated him like as if he would break. He should never have allowed her to dictate to him. He should have been up and about. Not lying in bed. That way made a man soft . . .

There were very few customers lolling at the bar of the Eldorado saloon when Buscadero arrived. He needed a drink badly. Betsy had nixed the idea of drink while he'd lain helpless under her ministrations. A drink would calm his nerves and what else he had in mind could be had here upstairs. It would take the starch out of him and put Betsy out of his mind, hopefully for good. Then, when he'd sloughed off Betsy's influence he was going to tread eggs carefully with Betsy so's not to hurt her feelings too much. Then he was going to ride out into the sunset . . . The plan was nearly too easy.

He nodded to the barman, then winked. Benny nodded. He was always on the lookout for clients for his girls. Nine out of ten customers wanted more than a beer. A beer or a shot of whisky got a man raring to go.

He got a glass and his best whisky and shot both along to where Buscadero was standing and they stopped precisely in front of the black-clad gunman. Benny prided himself on being a dead shot with glassess and bottles.

"You're lucky," he muttered. "You've gotta choice. Alice and Maria and the little blonde, Lucy . . . "

"Lucy?"

"Yeh, just started. She's taken Carrie's place. The bitch lit out . . . "

"I know. Lucy, now, is she any good?"

Benny shrugged. "She's young, if you like 'em young. Not much experience but willing."

"OK, It'll be Lucy. How much?"

"Ten dollars and two for her."

"Bloody hell! I can go down the road

and get two for that!"

"Suit yourself. Lucy's young and clean. We only have the best here," and Benny spat on a glass and then polished it.

Buscadero considered. Going with a whore was his way of getting Betsy out of his mind and easing the ache that had been building up for the past few days. Chre-ist! The sonofabitch barman must know he had a throb between his legs! It was extortion!

"Make it seven and you're on," and he eased the Colt hung low at his hip.

Benny saw the gesture and paused in the polishing of another glass. The threat was a delicate one, but you never knew with these visiting gun-hawks, and this one looked a mean sod.

"Right. But don't shoot your goddamn mouth off. I don't want a queue for cut-price pleasure! Up the stairs and the first on the right."

"Carrie's old room?"

"Yeh, the one you busted out of."

Benny grinned. "Come down by the stairs this time!"

Buscadero grinned ruefully back.

"I missed a good 'un, in Carrie?"

"Yeh, one of the best I've had. She brought the dough." Benny sighed. "I'd take her back tomorrow, but she's ambitious. Going back east and opening up a classy joint in Memphis or Atlanta if she can ever get that far. She will, I could lay bets on it."

"Well now, talking of Carrie won't do anything for me. I'll just go on up and make myself acquainted with the new girl."

"Yeh, just knock three times and she'll know she's gotta client."

Buscadero slowly mounted the stairs. He felt like an old man with about as much enthusiasm for it as an oldster. He could remember the time not so long ago when he would have taken the stairs two at a time and had his belt unbuckled before he was in the room. Still, Lucy would get the juices stirring. After all, he had the urge, it was only he didn't fancy a strange girl. His mind was still on Betsy.

Lucy was small and too damn young. Her bones were delicate and looked as if a man could crush her easily. Her naturally blonde hair was fine and curled like a baby's. She looked frightened. Christ! She should have still been with her mother. He swallowed. He'd made a bad mistake. He should have picked one of the big-titted ones.

"Hello, I'm known as Buscadero, and you're Lucy."

She nodded and nervously wet dry lips but didn't speak.

"What're you doing here, Lucy?"

"I'm . . . I'm . . . you can see what I'm doing!" and a desperate defiance flared a little anger into pale blue eyes bringing them alive. She was a pretty thing.

"You're new at it, aren't you?"

"What if I am? What's it to you? I'll do what you want . . ."

It was becoming clearer by the minute that Buscadero knew what he didn't want. Not this girl, not any girl. He was in the wrong place. He actually felt ashamed of himself. In some funny way he was letting Betsy down. Which was just bullshit. The sooner he put miles between him and Betsy the better and then he could resume his own life and enjoy a woman without this guilt shit, pay her and forget about it until the next time. That was the only way he could be free and enjoy life. After all, a bounty-hunting gunman who relied on his fast reflexes was neither a good insurance proposition nor good husband material. He sure wouldn't like to hurt any woman by being permanently attached to her. It wasn't fair expecting a woman to live day by day expecting to be a widow any time. No sir!

"What do you want to do?" and Buscadero came back to reality. Lucy was standing just in a shift which she held tightly about her neck as if to protect herself.

He looked about the small shabby room.

She nodded. "Benny let's us have a bottle of gutrot."

He pulled a face. "Pour me a shot. You have one too."

She shook her head. "I don't like it. Makes my head ache and I go to sleep and Benny gets mad."

She poured a generous measure into a glass for him and the bottle jiggled against the glass. By God, the kid was nearly wetting herself! A horrible thought struck him.

"I'm not the first? You *have* been with a man before?"

She hesitated and he groaned inwardly. He'd have Benny's guts for galluses.

"Yes. Of course I've done it before. I'm quite experienced. Really I am."

"Liar! You've probably done it once or twice with a boy in a haybarn and you think that's experience?"

She gulped. "Look, mister, what does it matter how much or how little I've done it? I'm willing. Now get on with it Benny will throw me out if I don't please you."

Buscadero drew a deep breath, swallowed the raw rotgut and poured another. Hell! He was feeling worse by the minute. He shook his head.

"I've changed my mind. I'm not in the mood. I'll pay you . . . " and he fumbled for the two dollars.

The girl sprang at him, twin spots of colour on her pale cheeks. She caught his hand.

"Mister, what's the matter with you? I told you I'm good." Her voice broke and suddenly tears were cascading down her cheeks. "Please, mister, if you go downstairs now, Benny will be furious. I'm new here and can only stay if I'm any good. I'll starve, mister, if he doesn't keep me on, and I don't want to go to those other places." She shuddered. "I've heard of what goes on in those other dives. They're worse than animals!"

"Haven't you got any folks?"

She shook her head, tears coming

again. "I had a brother, but he got shot. One of Maddison's men . . . he . . . he . . . wanted me and Mike was protecting me when it happened. I got no one else."

"How old are you?"

"Sixteen . . ."

Buscadero shook his head disbelievingly. She hastily told the truth.

"I'm nearly fifteen, but I don't see what difference it makes."

"It only makes me more determined to get you out of here."

"But it doesn't make sense! If you don't want me?"

"I know someone you can live with." He sighed. It meant not quite cutting the cords binding him to Betsy. If Betsy would take this kid under her wing he would have to keep sending money . . .

"But . . ."

"Look, kid, pack your things and we'll get out of here. I'll explain to Benny and make it worth his while to let you go without fuss."

Lucy's eyes blinked rapidly. Buscadero sighed again.

"Now don't you start that weeping again. I can't stand women who snivel!"

Lucy blew her nose and started a mad packing of a pitifully small amount of belongings which she stowed in a carpet-bag. She was soon finished. She put a battered bonnet on her head after shrugging on a snuff-coloured dress which covered her nakedness. Jesus! He would have to get Betsy to give her some drawers. Then winding herself about in a black shawl she stood submissively before him.

"I'm ready."

"Sure you haven't forgotten anything?"

"No. Never had much."

"Then we'll go."

She followed quietly when he walked along the bare passage and down the stairs. Benny poured beer for a customer and then watched them both, a frown on his face as he saw Lucy. His voice was brusque.

"And where the hell do you think you're going?"

Lucy looked frightened. "I'm going with him," and she nodded at Buscadero.

Benny's jaw dropped.

"That was bloody quick! Has she got something I didn't know about?" he asked the lounging Buscadero.

"She's certainly got something I like. I'm taking her with me."

"Oh, yeah? And what if I don't give the say-so? She works for me."

"I'm willing to pay."

"Yeh? How much?"

"Fifty dollars." Benny coughed and rasped his bristly chin. His little eyes gleamed. If she was worth fifty dollars to this sonofabitch, then maybe he was a fool to let her go. On the other hand, a lot of fellers didn't like the innocent flat-chested kind. Most men wanted raunchy women with big hips and bigger tits. Fifty dollars wasn't to be sneezed at . . .

"Make it seventy-five . . . ."

"Sixty."

"Done! Take her away and I hope she gives you the pox!"

Buscadero grinned. "And I hope someone shoots you in the balls!"

He put an arm about the girl and took her carpet-bag. Now all he had to do was persuade Betsy that she was a good Samaritan. Might be difficult owing to what he planned to do. But still . . .

They were moving to the batwings when they flung open and Betsy and Paul Maddison in a tangle of arms catapulted through the opening. Betsy's face was thunderous, as she struggled to pull his arm away from her throat. It looked as if her head would come clean off her shoulders. Paul's face was flushed, and the gun he held at her head wavered.

"So, I've found you, Buscadero. I'm going to kill you and then I'm gonna kill that other bastard for what you both did to my brother!"

Betsy made a wild effort to free herself.

"I'm sorry, Ed . . . Buscadero. He made me tell him where you would be. He threatened to shoot me in the stomach . . . "

"He did, did he?" and Buscadero's voice was cold and calm.

Lucy found herself spinning away and landed up sprawled across one of the tables. She quickly dropped and crawled underneath oblivious of bare arse and fleshy thighs. She waited and peeked from under cover. This black-clad stranger didn't seem fazed by the suddenness of the situation. She wondered if the girl was the one she was to live with.

Buscadero stood tense, his hands hovering near his low-slung guns. He'd hoped he could leave Greenwater Spring without incident. He certainly didn't want to face a wet-behind-the-ears kid who was keen to commit suicide . . .

"Son, your brother had it coming to him. My partner and I gave you a chance because you're just a kid. Go home and learn some sense!"

"Don't call me son," the boy snarled, "and I'm not a kid. I've been using a gun for years." Suddenly he flung Betsy from him and she made a dive for the table where Lucy crouched and joined her underneath. Paul eyed her briefly.

"I should have killed her too if she'd been stubborn, but I'll admit she had a raw deal with my brother and Cal Emmett. Where's Calorhan, Buscadero?"

"Gone. Lit out after a woman."

"So it's you and me, mister?"

"You're fighting drunk. Go home and sleep it off and you'll thank me tomorrow when you see the sun rise."

"I can take you, mister! You're not the only bastard who can fan a gun!"

"Then if you think so, boy, make your play!"

The boy's fingers flexed but he didn't draw. He hesitated and Buscadero smiled contemptuously. The piss-proud little bastard! He'd a good mind to draw and shoot his hat off and make the young fool crap himself! He needed a lesson in manners, how to shoot and how to carry his liquor . . . the arrogant little scumbag!

"What's the matter? Wakened up, have you? You're not dreaming, you know. Why don't you draw?" He knew he was goading the boy but he knew the yellow-spined sonofabitch was only mouthing off whipped-up-liquor bile.

"I'm not bluffing, you goddamn sadist! I'm just considering where I'll shoot you first. You made my brother suffer . . ."

"No sweat, boy. Aim for the kneecaps, then the belly. Have you ever seen a man with his guts shot out? A great place to smash a guy if you like to hear him scream. Go on, try your luck, boy. Make me yell, if you dare!"

He held his breath while the youth squirmed and twitched, his body shaking. Buscadero knew what was going through his mind. How the hate and lust for revenge was pouring through his veins like acid. Unless Paul

Maddison took the initiative, then it was going to be a classical stand-off, for Buscadero himself wouldn't pull a trigger on a teenage youth who should have been outside aiming at bottles.

Probably Buscadero was the first gunman he'd faced in anger.

The stupid bugger was working himself up to go for his gun . . .

He was actually going for it . . . the goddamn fool kid's fingers fumbled . . .

Buscadero's right hand moved in a blur and as he squeezed the trigger he was cursing lurid oaths at himself. He watched the crimson cover the shirt front and the body slowly sink to the floor.

He looked down at what remained of a reckless drunken youth. Hell! Why hadn't he shot to wing and not to kill? Because that was how he was trained. He could no more not shoot to kill, as stand and wait to be shot at.

He felt sick to his stomach.

This was the first time he'd shot a boy.

It was like shooting a wayward lamb.

He slammed his gun back into its holster. It was the first time he hadn't got a feeling of satisfaction out of a job well done. He hated himself for what he'd become.

It was time to ride out of Greenwater Spring and keep going.

He looked brusquely at Benny and all those who'd witnessed the shooting.

"You can explain what happened to the sheriff. It was self-defence."

Benny spat on the wooden plank floor and rubbed it with his toe into the grain.

"Some self-defence," he muttered, but he took care not to say it too loud.

★ ★ ★

Buscadero looked at the two girls. They were in the hotel bedroom. Betsy looked angry and Lucy looked close to tears.

"So there it is, Betsy. I figured you could look out for Lucy and I'll send you money from time to time. You can start up a school. You helped the schoolteacher Susie Mcgear so you know enough to teach the local kids. Lucy here can help you. She seems a bright little girl."

Betsy gave the shrinking girl a contemptuous look.

"I don't think I can teach her anything! Who'd want their kids being taught by someone who worked in the El Dorado? Hell! You have no understanding of folks, Buscadero!"

"Then I'll just have to take her along with me, and dump her on someone else, Betsy."

"Now wait. Don't be hasty. Maybe I could find her a job on some ranch. There's women wanting help with kids and all that."

"Well, you do that, Betsy, and we'll keep in touch."

"But you're not fit enough to ride out, Ed . . ."

"For hell's sake, don't call me that!"

Lucy looked interested. Buscadero

was angry. He could paddle Betsy's behind. He took a deep breath.

"Davey never knew what a complicated thing he was doing when he got me to promise to give you seventy-four dollars and sixty-five cents!"

"Look, Buscadero, promise you'll stay another couple of days?"

"Why? The situation will be just the same. No, I've made my mind up, Betsy. I'm on my way as soon as I've got my supplies."

"Where are you heading for?"

He shrugged. "I don't know. Maybe take off after Jack Calorhan. But I wouldn't tell you if I knew!"

"But you'll send an address when you send Lucy some money?"

"You can trust me on that, Betsy. I'll see you both right."

Betsy nodded and then surprisingly caught Lucy by-the arm.

"We'll leave now, Lucy, and we'll go shopping. I think you could do with some new clothes and mine are far too big for you."

Buscadero looked suspiciously at Betsy. She was taking this all too quietly. He'd expected hysterics and tears at the very least. Maybe he'd figured her wrong. He wasn't an expert on women of her kind. Barring her treatment at the hands of Maddison and his gang and the one brief episode with himself that made him tingle when he thought of it, she was a respectable girl but with a deep capacity for love. A rare combination indeed, if all the husbands he'd talked to were to be believed.

"Betsy, I'll be gone when you get back."

"Will you, Buscadero?" She sounded to damn casual. He was piqued.

"Where'll I send the money?"

"Here at the hotel. I'll get it, Buscadero, and I'll see Lucy gets it."

"You'll keep some for yourself?"

"If you want me to, Buscadero."

"Right. That's it, then?"

"Right. Thanks for bringing me Father's money. I appreciate it."

"Right. Well, this is goodbye and to you too, Lucy."

Lucy blinked, the ready tears threatening to spill over. They irritated Buscadero. Chre-ist! She had some growing up to do. Men hated women who cried.

"Goodbye, Buscadero, and thank you for getting me out of that place. I'll do everything Betsy tells me."

"Good. I want you two to be friends. Goodbye, Betsy," and Buscadero held out his hand but Betsy studiously looked away from him.

"Goodbye. Come on, Lucy, let's get those doo-dars for you," and she actually walked out of the bedroom and never gave Buscadero another glance.

"Phoo! Women!" Buscadero said aloud. "Can you beat that?" and shook his head. He would never understand nice women . . .

He wasn't prepared for the nasty feeling in his stomach. It was a lonely hollow feeling that he couldn't relate to. He'd never had it before. If he didn't know better, he would have described it as missing the infuriating wench!

He gathered his belongings and stuffed them into his warbag, then went down and paid his bill.

"When does the next train to Abilene go through?"

The hotel-keeper studied a flyblown timetable.

"There's a mail-train goes just to Abilene passing through here at six tonight. You've gotta change at Abilene for points east."

"Good. I'll make it easy. Thanks for everything, old timer. I'll recommend you to my friends." The old man's faded blue eyes lit up and then dulled again.

"Shucks!" he said bad-temperedly, "You aint' got no friends!"

Buscadero grinned and patted him on the shoulder. "Anyway, thanks for letting me stay with a bullet in my shoulder."

The man nodded and watched the

tall black-clad figure leave his premises. He sighed with relief. He didn't like well known gunhawks on his premises. He'd been lucky. No one had come to try the feller out. Not like at his friend Benny's place when the bastard had shot that boy and there'd been blood everywhere . . .

★ ★ ★

Buscadero saw his horse was comfortable in the boxcar with dry straw and plenty of hay to chew on and then made his way to the passengers' section and sat down at a window-seat after loosening his belt and making himself easy.

The strange mood was still on him. For once in his life he wasn't sure of doing the right thing. Usually he could make his mind up about what he should do or where he should go. But now his mind was in a turmoil. Blast coming back to where your roots were! It unsettled a lifetime of routine.

He gazed moodily at the countryside

as the train cranked itself up for the half-day run to Abilene. He would have to make his mind up there whether he went on east or stayed on in the Territory. Maybe he would make for Kansas City . . .

He remembered his plan to go to Montana and raise horses. But that meant settling down. Aw, to hell!

He slept most of the way to Abilene. There were no incidents, no excitements like train-robbers or such. Maybe this mail-train didn't carry enough to hold the train up for. Train-robbers were mighty careful these days what with the telegraph and all.

He awakened with a start. The old train was slowing down. He could feel the scrape of the brakes on the track. He poked his head out of the window and inhaled a cloud of black smoke and dust. He coughed. But he'd seen the huddle of buildings on both sides of the track. They were coming into Abilene. It was just as well. His arse had corns from sitting on the hard wooden seat. It would have been a better ride on horseback. He gathered his warbag and his rifle and the pouch he carried his ammunition in. It wasn't much in the way of baggage for a man to show after twenty years but he comforted himself with the thought of that tidy sum in the New York bank which was waiting for the day which he hoped was a long ways off when he would retire in earnest. It was nice to know it was steadily growing. He wouldn't be an old down-and-out when his bones started to creak.

He opened the carriage door to step down when the last blast of the engine's whistle announced its arrival. He was the only one in the doorway. He shouldered his bags but before he could take a step down three men stepped forward.

He eyed them curiously. All looked a little uncomfortable. The smallest fattest one spoke up.

"I'm Sheriff Daly and these are my

deputies. We've got a warrant for your arrest."

Buscadero goggled. What the hell . . . ?

"I think there's some mistake. You've got the wrong man."

"No mistake, mister. We gotta telegraph about you. You're Buscadero? A man all in black six feet four, weighs close on two hundred and fifty . . . "

"Cut the crap! I'm Buscadero all right. But I'm on no wanted lists. There's some mistake!"

"I'm afraid you'll have to come along with us. You gotta horse?"

"Yes. I should be back there unloading him."

"Chas, nip off like a good lad and see to it." The tall silent youth beside him nodded.

"Yes, Paw. I'll get him. A roan the telegraph said?" The older man nodded.

Buscadero stared.

"Jesus, Joseph and Mary! Just what is this?"

"You'll find out. The mayor's waiting

for you at the Railway Hotel."

Suddenly Buscadero thought of Jack Calorhan. This was some joke of Jack's!

"You're a friend of Jack Calorhan? Jeeze! I might have known it." The sheriff looked blank.

"Never heard of the guy."

"Then what . . . ?"

"You'll know soon enough, feller," and without another word, Buscadero was led away between the sheriff and his remaining deputy. He considered breaking free and then reason took over. Why should he? He'd done nothing wrong and he'd most likely lose his horse and that wasn't to be thought of.

He resigned himself to having the patience to find out what it was all about.

They marched him to the jail and though he protested they locked him in a cell on his own, and apart from feeding him a damn good supper no one came to look him over.

He'd have someone's guts for galluses tomorrow!

The next day passed slowly and apart from his being fed at intervals, the sheriff and the mayor didn't have the guts to come and face his wrath. Buscadero amused himself rustling up new ways on how to kill a man with a hundred cuts of a knife.

Finally there was the noise of many voices in the next room and then the scrape of a key in the cell block and the heavy door swung open, and a pair of light feminine boots clattered across the stone-flagged floor, and Betsy was hanging on to the bars and looking at him with the sheriff and a strange man in silver wire-rimmed spectacles peering at him from the rear.

"Yes, that's him, Sheriff. The thieving two-timing blackguard!" and incredibly, Betsy started to sob.

"Betsy! What the hell's going on?"

"There, you see, he knows me! If it wasn't for the baby, I wouldn't pursue him," and Betsy pulled out a handkerchief and buried her nose in it.

The sheriff and the stranger made soft sympathetic sounds, the sheriff glaring at Buscadero.

"You should be ashamed of yourself, young man. Taking this lady's money and that of her young sister and leaving them in the wilderness, and her expecting your child!"

Buscadero stared.

"But . . . " For once he had nothing to say. His wits were frozen.

"Eddie, promise you'll marry me, and Daddy will forgive us all. Think of poor Lucy, who sided with us. She knows how we love each other. Daddy will relent when he sees how happy we are and when he knows about the baby, he'll make me his heir again, I promise you!"

Buscadero swallowed. She was a bloody good actress and he would have laughed if it hadn't been so serious.

"Darling, why don't you say something? You know you love me. These kind folks have arranged for the preacher . . . "

"Yes, now, young man, you don't know how lucky you be," the sheriff went on severely. "This beautiful young lady is aching to be your wife. Now make an honest woman of her or the mayor here who also happens to be a judge will convene a court and we'll find plenty of charges to put you away for seven years. Now which is it to be, son?"

"I suppose I haven't any choice."

The sheriff showed tobacco-stained teeth.

"Not two happy choices, son. Now if I was you, I'd settle for a life sentence with the little woman," and he grinned at his own wit.

Buscadero stared at him, unable to enjoy the joke. He could feel an invisible rope fastening him and Betsy together. He had a momentary panicky sense of being trapped like some jack rabbit.

Then he looked at Betsy, and he could see love and doubt and determination in her eyes. It struck him that if she was having a baby, then it might well be someone else's.

He couldn't betray her to these strangers. The kidnapping and rape hadn't been her fault. On the other hand if she'd been a whore, then she would have known how to protect herself.

He sighed.

He closed his eyes. If he wanted her he would have taken her irrespective of whose child it was.

Could he do that and not come to hate her for trapping him into marriage?

He remembered their night together.

"Well, son, we're waiting."

Funny how he'd called young Paul Maddison, son, in that same condescending way, and now this old buzzard was calling him son. Chre-ist! He coughed. The words were hard to get out. He looked full into her eyes.

"Betsy, will you marry me?" and saw the flash of joy quickly repressed.

"If you really want me, Buscadero."

"Now what kind of an answer is that?" the little sheriff roared. "Damme! Let's get him in front of the preacher before she changes her mind. Let's think of the baby, shall we?"

The keys were found and the barred cell door opened and Buscadero found himself hustled out of the jail and down Main Street with the sheriff and deputies in close attendance as if he still might take off and make his escape.

Then he was standing in front of a white-haired preacher and his fat dumpy wife and incredibly he was repeating words and phrases he thought he would never use. Then in a daze he turned to Betsy.

"Well, how do you feel now, Mrs Juantes?"

Betsy flung her arms about his neck and her kiss told him she was thrilled, and Lucy cried as a bridesmaid should and the young deputy held her hand and offered her a big red handkerchief.

The sheriff blew his nose. All this

reminded him of his own young bride of forty years ago. There had been no indication then that she would become a nagging wife. He didn't know whether to congratulate or commiserate with the fine upstanding man in black. He looked strong enough to fight the good fight with his bride. But there was one thing certain. She'd won the first round.

* * *

Later that night, Buscadero and Betsy watched the moon rise. It's pale silvery light cast blue shadows and made the sun-bleached jumble that made up Abilene much more beautiful than during the raw sun-drenched hours.

They'd talked and made love and it was how he'd remembered it. Perhaps marriage wasn't going to be so bad after all. Now, as passion was for the time slaked, he could broach that which had been on his mind ever since they'd left the preacher's house.

"Betsy, did you know you were in the family way when we first made love?"

Betsy hung her head and he could see her eyelashes heavy on her cheeks. He put out a finger and lefted her chin.

"Betsy?"

He was surprised to see her eyes crystal-bright as if tears were ready to spill. "Betsy, what is it, my dear? You can tell me anything. I'm your husband, remember?"

She blinked rapidly and then bit her lip.

"Promise you won't be angry?"

"Why should I be. I already know there's the probability that the child will be a Maddison or an Emmett or whoever. How many men were there, Betsy?"

Betsy swallowed.

"Six." Something clutched his heart. "That many?" She nodded.

"It could be any of them."

"I didn't say that. You asked me how

many raped me. Six. Do you hate me for it, Edward?"

"It wasn't your fault," he answered gruffly but it was something he wanted to forget.

"You could have told the sheriff when you were in the jail, the baby might not be yours."

"But that would have made you out to be a whore and you're never that, Betsy, love."

Something didn't sound quite right. He was aware of something but not what it was. There was something inconsistent . . . and then he grabbed her. Of course!

"Betsy, stop playing games with me. You said six, so the baby has a choice of six fathers, but when I said six, you said and I quote, *you asked me how many raped me.* What did you mean?"

Then incredibly she was crying and leaning her head on his shoulder. He felt sick. Hell! If she'd been with a lover before being raped, he would kill that man! She was *his* wife, and there wasn't going to be another man alive who'd been loved by her . . .

He shook her until her head nearly snapped from her shoulders.

"Answer me, you stupid bitch, or I'll finish you! Who was he?"

"There isn't any baby," she wept. "I only made that up to make the sheriff haul you in. I was frightened I was going to lose you!"

"You mean it was all a trap to get me hogtied?"

"Yes!" she yelled in her fear of what he would do. "I didn't want you to ride away and leave me. I'd do it again if I had to!" She finished on a note of defiance.

For a long long moment there was complete silence and she squirmed under his tightening hold while relief and then a curious kind of disappointment went through him. So there was no baby . . . Then exultation coursed through him as the shock and tension left him. His roar made her jump like a gazelle ready for flight.

"You scheming little bitch! I should paddle your arse!" His mouth came down on hers and her fear turned to wonder and then delight. When she came up for air she said softly,

"Do you still want to paddle my arse?"

"Hmm . . . let's go to bed."

"And after that?"

"We'll talk about going to Montana and raising horses."

"And kids?"

"Of course. Kids and horses, in that order."

"Then come on, we'd best get some practice in. It's a long way to Montana!"

TOP HAND
Wade Everett

The Broken T was big. But no ranch is big enough to let a man hide from himself.

GUN WOLVES OF LOBO BASIN
Lee Floren

The Feud was a blood debt. When Smoke Talbot found the outlaws who gunned down his folks he aimed to nail their hide to the barn door.

SHOTGUN SHARKEY
Marshall Grover

The westbound coach carrying the indomitable Larry and Stretch headed for a shooting showdown.

FIGHTING RAMROD
Charles N. Heckelmann

Most men would have cut their losses, but Frazer counted the bullets in his guns and said he'd soak the range in blood before he'd give up another inch of what was his.

LONE GUN
Eric Allen

Smoke Blackbird had been away too long. The Lequires had seized the Blackbird farm, forcing the Indians and settlers off, and no one seemed willing to fight! He had to fight alone.

THE THIRD RIDER
Barry Cord

Mel Rawlins wasn't going to let anything stand in his way. His father was murdered, his two brothers gone. Now Mel rode for vengeance.

ARIZONA DRIFTERS
W. C. Tuttle

When drifting Dutton and Lonnie Steelman decide to become partners they find that they have a common enemy in the formidable Thurston brothers.

TOMBSTONE
Matt Braun

Wells Fargo paid Luke Starbuck to outgun the silver-thieving stagecoach gang at Tombstone. Before long Luke can see the only thing bearing fruit in this eldorado will be the gallows tree.

HIGH BORDER RIDERS
Lee Floren

Buckshot McKee and Tortilla Joe cut the trail of a border tough who was running Mexican beef into Texas. They stopped the smuggler in his tracks.

BRETT RANDALL, GAMBLER
E. B. Mann

Larry Day had the choice of running away from the law or of assuming a dead man's place. No matter what he decided he was bound to end up dead.

THE GUNSHARP
William R. Cox

The Eggerleys weren't very smart. They trained their sights on Will Carney and Arizona's biggest blood bath began.

THE DEPUTY OF SAN RIANO
Lawrence A. Keating and
Al. P. Nelson

When a man fell dead from his horse, Ed Grant was spotted riding away from the scene. The deputy sheriff rode out after him and came up against everything from gunfire to dynamite.

FARGO: MASSACRE RIVER
John Benteen

The ambushers up ahead had now blocked the road. Fargo's convoy was a jumble, a perfect target for the insurgents' weapons!

SUNDANCE: DEATH IN THE LAVA
John Benteen

The Modoc's captured the wagon train and its cargo of gold. But now the halfbreed they called Sundance was going after it . . .

HARSH RECKONING
Phil Ketchum

Five years of keeping himself alive in a brutal prison had made Brand tough and careless about who he gunned down . . .

FARGO: PANAMA GOLD
John Benteen

With foreign money behind him, Buckner was going to destroy the Panama Canal before it could be completed. Fargo's job was to stop Buckner.

FARGO: THE SHARPSHOOTERS
John Benteen

The Canfield clan, thirty strong were raising hell in Texas. Fargo was tough enough to hold his own against the whole clan.

PISTOL LAW
Paul Evan Lehman

Lance Jones came back to Mustang for just one thing — revenge! Revenge on the people who had him thrown in jail.

HELL RIDERS
Steve Mensing

Wade Walker's kid brother, Duane, was locked up in the Silver City jail facing a rope at dawn. Wade was a ruthless outlaw, but he was smart, and he had vowed to have his brother out of jail before morning!

DESERT OF THE DAMNED
Nelson Nye

The law was after him for the murder of a marshal — a murder he didn't commit. Breen was after him for revenge — and Breen wouldn't stop at anything . . . blackmail, a frameup . . . or murder.

DAY OF THE COMANCHEROS
Steven C. Lawrence

Their very name struck terror into men's hearts — the Comancheros, a savage army of cutthroats who swept across Texas, leaving behind a bloodstained trail of robbery and murder.

SUNDANCE: SILENT ENEMY
John Benteen

A lone crazed Cheyenne was on a personal war path. They needed to pit one man against one crazed Indian. That man was Sundance.

LASSITER
Jack Slade

Lassiter wasn't the kind of man to listen to reason. Cross him once and he'll hold a grudge for years to come — if he let you live that long.

LAST STAGE TO GOMORRAH
Barry Cord

Jeff Carter, tough ex-riverboat gambler, now had himself a horse ranch that kept him free from gunfights and card games. Until Sturvesant of Wells Fargo showed up.

McALLISTER ON THE COMANCHE CROSSING
Matt Chisholm

The Comanche, McAllister owes them a life — and the trail is soaked with the blood of the men who had tried to outrun them before.

QUICK-TRIGGER COUNTRY
Clem Colt

Turkey Red hooked up with Curly Bill Graham's outlaw crew. But wholesale murder was out of Turk's line, so when range war flared he bucked the whole border gang alone . . .

CAMPAIGNING
Jim Miller

Ambushed on the Santa Fe trail, Sean Callahan is saved by two Indian strangers. But there'll be more lead and arrows flying before the band join Kit Carson against the Comanches.

GUNSLINGER'S RANGE
Jackson Cole

Three escaped convicts are out for revenge. They won't rest until they put a bullet through the head of the dirty snake who locked them behind bars.

RUSTLER'S TRAIL
Lee Floren

Jim Carlin knew he would have to stand up and fight because he had staked his claim right in the middle of Big Ike Outland's best grass.

THE TRUTH ABOUT SNAKE RIDGE
Marshall Grover

The troubleshooters came to San Cristobal to help the needy. For Larry and Stretch the turmoil began with a brawl and then an ambush.

WOLF DOG RANGE
Lee Floren

Will Ardery would stop at nothing, unless something stopped him first — like a bullet from Pete Manly's gun.

DEVIL'S DINERO
Marshall Grover

Plagued by remorse, a rich old reprobate hired the Texas Troubleshooters to deliver a fortune in greenbacks to each of his victims.

GUNS OF FURY
Ernest Haycox

Dane Starr, alias Dan Smith, wanted to close the door on his past and hang up his guns, but people wouldn't let him.

DONOVAN
Elmer Kelton

Donovan was supposed to be dead. Uncle Joe Vickers had fired off both barrels of a shotgun into the vicious outlaw's face as he was escaping from jail. Now Uncle Joe had been shot — in just the same way.

CODE OF THE GUN
Gordon D. Shirreffs

MacLean came riding home, with saddle tramp written all over him, but sewn in his shirt-lining was an Arizona Ranger's star.

GAMBLER'S GUN LUCK
Brett Austen

Gamblers seldom live long. Parker was a hell of a gambler. It was his life — or his death . . .

ORPHAN'S PREFERRED
Jim Miller

Sean Callahan answers the call of the Pony Express and fights Indians and outlaws to get the mail through.

DAY OF THE BUZZARD
T. V. Olsen

All Val Penmark cared about was getting the men who killed his wife.

THE MANHUNTER
Gordon D. Shirreffs

Lee Kershaw knew that every Rurale in the territory was on the lookout for him. But the offer of $5,000 in gold to find five small pieces of leather was too good to turn down.

RIFLES ON THE RANGE
Lee Floren

Doc Mike and the farmer stood there alone between Smith and Watson. There was this moment of stillness, and then the roar would start. And somebody would die . . .

HARTIGAN
Marshall Grover

Hartigan had come to Cornerstone to die. He chose the time and the place, and Main Street became a battlefield.

SUNDANCE: OVERKILL
John Benteen

When a wealthy banker's daughter was kidnapped by the Cheyenne, he offered Sundance $10,000 to rescue the girl.